PICK-UP GAME

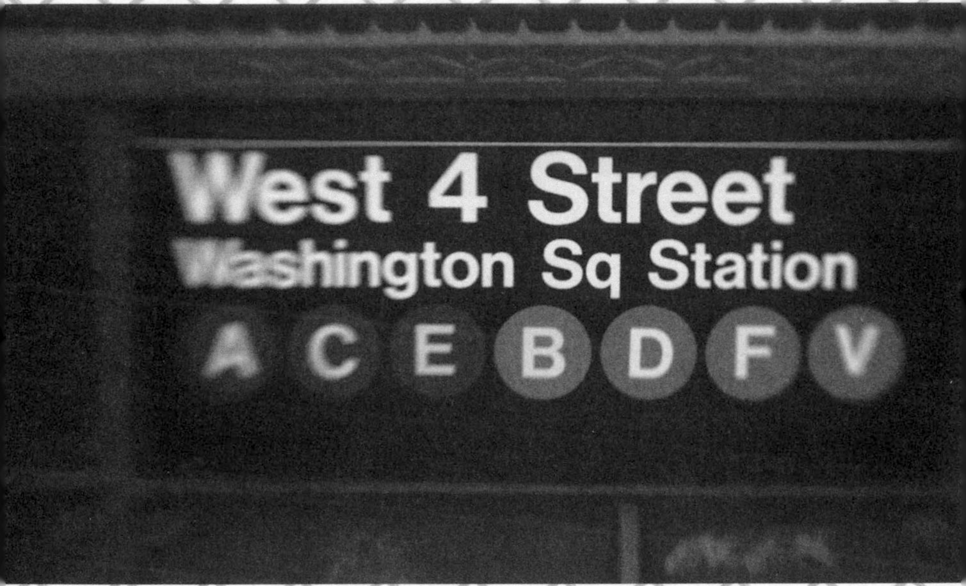
West 4 Street
Washington Sq Station
A C E B D F V

PICK-UP
GAME
A FULL
DAY OF
FULL
COURT

edited by

Marc Aronson and Charles R. Smith Jr.

CANDLEWICK PRESS

Compilation copyright © 2011
by Marc Aronson and Charles R. Smith Jr.
Photographs copyright © 2011 by Charles R. Smith Jr.
"Step into the Arena," "Next," "My Boys," "Wild Cats,"
"El Profesor," "The Fire Inside," "Back in the Day," "24/7,"
and "Represent" copyright © 2011 by Charles R. Smith Jr.
"Cage Run" copyright © 2011 by Walter Dean Myers
"Laws of Motion" copyright © 2011 by Bruce Brooks
"Mira Mira" copyright © 2011 by Willie Perdomo
"Virgins Are Lucky" copyright © 2011 by Sharon G. Flake
"Practice Don't Make Perfect" copyright © 2011 by Robert Burleigh
"He's Gotta Have It" copyright © 2011 by Rita Williams-Garcia
"Head Game" copyright © 2011 by Joseph Bruchac
"Just Shane" copyright © 2011 by Adam Rapp
"The Shoot" copyright © 2011 by Robert Lipsyte
Afterword copyright © 2011 by Marc Aronson

First paperback edition 2012

The Library of Congress has cataloged the hardcover edition as follows:
The pick-up game / edited by Marc Aronson & Charles R. Smith.
— 1st ed.
p. cm.
Summary: A series of short stories by such authors as Walter Dean
Myers, Rita Williams-Garcia, and Joseph Bruchac, interspersed
with poems and photographs, provides different perspectives
on a game of streetball played one steamy July day at the
West 4th Street court in New York City known as The Cage.
ISBN 978-0-7636-4562-5 (hardcover)
[1. Basketball—Fiction. 2. Interpersonal relations—Fiction.
3. African Americans—Fiction. 4. New York (N.Y.)—Fiction.]
I. Aronson, Marc. II. Smith, Charles R., date.
PZ5.P55 2011
[Fic]—dc22 2010038694

ISBN 978-0-7636-6068-0 (paperback)

12 13 14 15 16 17 BVG 10 9 8 7 6 5 4 3 2 1

Printed in Berryville, VA, U.S.A.

This book was typeset in ITC Mendoza.

Candlewick Press
99 Dover Street
Somerville, Massachusetts 02144

visit us at www.candlewick.com

To the players and coaches
who taught me to box out
and hustle back
and move your feet—
enjoy the game.

M. A.

This is for
the ankle-breakers,
the circus-shot makers,
the made-you-look
got-you-shook
smooth shake-and-bakers,
the twine-twisters,
free-throw-line dishers,
the from-the-corner stop-and-pop
sit-you-down-swishers,
and all those who love them.

C. R. S.

STEP INTO THE ARENA

Charles R. Smith Jr.

9:12 A.M.

Step into the arena
where gladiators meet,
the Cage at West 4th,
home of hallowed concrete,
where ballers test skill,
heart
soul
and will,
and go toe-to-toe
to entertain
and thrill
faces behind fences
focused courtside
on warriors being tested
with noplace to hide.
Battle-hardened bodies
crash into the fence
from "no blood, no foul"
hands-on defense,
making wide-eyed wannabes
freeze and get shook,
'cause here you show heart
or your soul
will get took.

CAGE RUN

Walter Dean Myers

"Boo, you wake?" Moms standing in the doorway.

"Yeah."

"That white boy on the phone," she said. "What he want calling so early?"

"What white boy?"

"The one brought that little skinny girl up here last week."

"Fish," I said. "I don't know what he wants."

"He going to marry that girl?"

"I don't know, Mom."

The minutes on my cell were long gone, and so I had to trek out to the kitchen to use the house phone. Shanay was up, looking at something in a bowl. I asked her what she was eating.

"Grits," she said. "You want some?"

"Naw," I said as I picked up the phone. "Yo, Fish, what's up, man?"

"You want to run tomorrow morning?" he asked. "I got some dudes together. Maybe about nine? Down at the Cage."

"Nine in the damned morning?" I asked. "Who's going to be running at nine in the morning?"

"Some of my guys got jobs," Fish said. "I figured we could get in a good run, five-on-five, for twenty cents a man. Cop some exercise."

Whoa. The alarms went off big-time Jeff Fisher loved ball and knew I was into balling, but why was he trying to sweeten the pot? He wouldn't be calling me the first thing in the morning talking about running no ball for twenty dollars a man unless there was something going on.

"I don't know, man," I said. "Nine is early. This is July. Guys don't want to get out of bed that time."

"You can't handle it?" he asked. Calm. Casual. That was Fish.

"Give me a minute and call me back," I said.

Fish and me have played ball together since the fifth grade. He was a run-mouth and had the game to back it up. But if there was any taste involved, it would usually be three dollars, maybe five at the most, enough to buy some sodas. Him talking about twenty dollars a man meant he was really anxious to get something going. I asked Shanay if I could use her cell.

"No."

I called my man Earl on my mother's phone.

"I think he's going to bring down some white boys from college," Earl said. "They got that kind of money to be throwing around. Or maybe he got some of them wine heads he play with out at St. John's in Brooklyn. They beat you half to death."

"Yeah, but they can't run with us and Fish knows that," I said. "He got something else going on if he's going to lay out twenty a man and don't even ask me who I'm going to bring."

"Yeah, but it don't make me no nevermind because I ain't got twenty dollars anyway," Earl said.

"Ronnie got money," I said. "We get him to front us, we can play. We just got to figure out what Fish got up his sleeve."

"If Ronnie is fronting, I'm in," Earl said.

Earl had played some football and looked it. Thick head, thick neck that came down into sloping shoulders, and a body that tapered quickly into a small waistline that moved a lot quicker than people expected. Most of all he hated to lose and was as strong as skunk pee. He was half the battle.

I called around and lined up Jamal, Ronnie from 116th Street, and LD, a skinny brother with a nice touch. Ronnie agreed to front the deal, but he was worried about Fish, too.

"He knows that we know he's slick, and it don't even matter to him," Ronnie said. "But what I think is he's got some big center and he thinks we won't know who he is. It's got to be a size thing. If everybody shows up, we can handle our business."

Like Ronnie said, Fish was throwing down and we all knew it. But that was the challenge, and I was hooked.

Mom asked me what Fish had wanted, and I told her we were going to be playing ball in the morning. She asked me if Mr. Morton, my coach, knew about it, and I said something about "Yeah, Tiny knows." She could smell the lie but didn't push it.

LD lived with his aunt on St. Nicholas Ave., and by eight fifteen in the morning, we were piling into the A train ready to go down to West 4th. On the way, everybody was talking about how we were going to bust some serious ass and how it really didn't mean nothing who Fish brought. I wasn't buying that because I had known Fish for longer than the other guys, and me and him were close. The skinny girl he had brought to the house was Marilyn, and he had brought her around for my moms to check her out because he was dead-on serious about marrying her.

"You ain't but seventeen," my moms had said to him. "If she ain't pregnant, why you in such a hurry?"

Fish said he was in love but the real reason was that Marilyn was the only decent white chick he knew.

The Cage. I loved the place. A tiny little court surrounded by a twenty-foot fence that every real player in the city knew about and eventually showed up with their best game to be checked out. It was as if we were all gladiators coming into the arena to show off our skills. We got off at the 8th Street exit and walked slowly down 6th Avenue to 4th. I could feel myself getting excited and could hear Jamal's voice start getting high. He was excited, too. Soon as we got close, we spotted Fish talking to Marcus from Fort Greene.

"Marcus can't handle me," LD said. "I'll eat his ass up."

I knew Marcus, too, and he was OK. He had a nice jump shot if you gave him room to set it up. Him and Fish were both good shooters, and I figured that if they did have a monster to fill the paint, that might be the play.

"Hey, Fish, what's happening, my brother!" I gave Fish a fist bump.

"What's happening, Mr. Byron Jackson?" Fish came back. "How's the family and especially sweet little Shantay?"

"Don't be looking at my sister," I said. "I'll have to get my shotgun out."

"I got to change my shoelaces," Jamal said. "The left one broke and it's bad luck to wear different shoelaces."

"Your bad luck started when you showed up," Fish said. "The shoelaces won't help."

"Well, we gonna see, white boy," Jamal said. "That's why we here."

Jamal knew his shoelace wasn't broken, but we wanted to get some time to assess who they had and strategize.

"Who they got?" Jamal was asking when we reached the sideline. "Fish and Marcus can play, but they ain't all that."

"Yo, Boo, I played against that light-skinned guy with FLYER across his shirt," Earl said to me. "His name is Bryan."

"How he play?" I asked.

"He's pretty good," Earl said. "He can get up and snatch bounds, but he's too skinny to make a difference. And that dude with all the muscle is Frankie Walls. He's starting for Grady this year. He looks strong, but my grandmother got more speed."

"Who's that other white guy they got?" Jamal asked. "I think he's a white supremacist or something."

We looked over and saw the guy Jamal was talking about. He was about my height, six two . . . maybe six three, with square, bony shoulders. Kind of a creepy-looking dude.

"Why you think he's a white supremacist?" I asked.

"Look how white the sucker is," Jamal said. "You know he must have been in prison or something. He ain't never been in no sun."

"He's wearing a sweatshirt," Earl said. "If he takes it off, we can see if he's got any tats. All those skinheads got tats and shit."

"No, man, he wouldn't be hanging out with Fish if he was a skinhead," I said. "They don't like Jews either."

"He got to be their ace," Jamal said. "Unless they wouldn't be throwing no twenty dollars in the pot."

"We'll find out." LD was pulling on his jockstrap. "And it really don't make me no nevermind. I'm going home with some money today."

I knew it wasn't about the paper. Fish had just thrown that in to make sure I could get guys down so early in the morning. There was something else floating around in his head.

Fish had brought along three brothers and the pale white dude to take us on. When he introduced us, he said the white guy's name was Waco. Up close he didn't look like a ballplayer. His eyes were set deep and looked dark, but that could have been just because he was so pale. He had dirty blond hair that hung down over his forehead and a thin mouth that looked like somebody had just slashed it across his face. But the thing that set him apart was how white he was. He wasn't like an albino because his eyes were dark enough. It was just that he didn't have any color to him, and I was wondering if he was a crackhead or something, and if he was, what the heck Fish was hanging with him for.

We were going to go eleven, straight. We got two Korean students with NYU backpacks to keep score for us so there would be no arguments.

OK, I know my game is correct. Fish was hip to everybody on my squad, and when he told us to take the ball out first, I knew he was making the matchups.

The run started out cool enough, and right away I saw that Waco was on me. I figured Fish had told him about my game, but telling and smelling ain't the same, so I wasn't worried.

He picked me up just past the short half court line they got in the Cage and started pushing me toward the side. That was cool. White college ball 101; don't give your man the middle. I gave up the ball to Jamal and went to set up a screen, but Waco was on my case and blocking it off. I stepped to him, pushed off, and went to the corner, where I got the ball and went up for the shot.

The shot dropped, and we had to stop the game to figure out if we were going to go with threes or not. We had the size so I said no and Fish went along with it.

They brought the ball down, and Waco was off the play and sliding toward the corner. I thought he was going to either come in and bump back out to the corner to match my shot or try to cut across the lane to see what he could do there.

He did come in, bumped out a step, and then posted high when the ball swung away from us. Fish made a move to the hoop and passed out to Waco. He went straight up without faking or putting the ball on the ground. Efficient. He dropped his shot, and I could see he was confident. I tightened up on him, and he was on me just as hard. He ran his hands good, first a hand on my side, then on my hip; he was watching the ball and feeling where I was at the same time. When I was on the dribble, he played back just enough where the crossover wasn't going to work but not too far back for me to get off another easy jumper.

On one play, we got into some serious Cage play. Marcus tried to hand check LD and got knocked hard into the fence, making a girl leaning against the fence drop her ice cream. I liked that.

The game was going back and forth, and I thought everybody was on their game when Ronnie called time-out.

"Yo, Boo, get into it, man!" he said to me. "I got some bucks on the game. They're ahead, and you ain't getting with it."

"Dude's all over me," I said. "You see I ain't free."

"Bruise his ass!" was the comeback.

Ronnie was right. I had to give Waco a heart check.

Earl was leaning against the fence when he threw the ball in to LD.

"Look for me on the breakaway," I said. "Alley left!"

LD passed the ball to Jamal, who brought it down, and I headed right toward the center. Like I figured, Waco came out and blocked off the middle, waiting for me to pick a side. No way. I made a little jive fake to my right, which I knew he wasn't going to go for, and then went right at him, planting my right foot on top of his right sneaker hard and pushing off straight past him. I knew with my foot on his, he couldn't move, and by the time he got turned around, I was down the left side and going up for Jamal's pass.

There weren't many people watching the game when I came down from the slam, but it made me feel good. When I went back upcourt, I brushed past Waco like he was nothing.

He had been trying to post me, which I thought was wack because he didn't know how strong I am. He tried to push in down the lane again with Flyer on the other line. They were taking turns rocking toward the middle and looking for the pass. Waco was steady backing into me and he was strong, but I brought my elbow up aside his head, all the time looking the other way like I didn't know I was up in his face. When the ball came in to Flyer and he spun into the middle with a little left-hand move, I clocked Waco out hard.

He whirled toward me as Earl grabbed the bound and started downcourt.

"What? *What?*" I stood toe-to-toe and eyeball-to-eyeball with the sucker. "You got something to say?"

He didn't say nothing. He just lifted his hands in the air a little like, "Hey, if that's the game . . ." He went on to midcourt and didn't turn until the ball came out from under the basket and Jamal was setting us up again.

Fish had seen me and Waco facing off and looked at both of us but he didn't say nothing either. I would have thought that maybe the game was over, that I had just punked Waco out and we were on the way to copping the game except for one thing: when me and him were face-to-face and I could feel the dude's breath on me, it was like, seriously cold. We were in the middle of the damned summer running a full and the dude's breath was cold as freaking ice. He was sweating; I could see the drops on his brow, but he was still pale and his breath was flat-out cold.

It was 7–6 in their favor; by now there were more people watching the game and about at least a half dozen guys who wanted to get some game. A fat brother was selling water near the entrance to the

Cage for two dollars a bottle, and I saw Fish standing with him. I went over.

"Yo, Boo, let's not get into nothing," Fish said.

"That guy got some kind of disease or something?" I asked Fish. "His breath is cold, man. What's up with that?"

"No, he's OK," Fish said. He looked away and then glanced past my shoulder to where Waco was leaning against the fence. "He's from out in River-head, where my cousin lives. I played some ball with him out there, and I liked the game and gave him my number. I kind of owe him. You know what I mean?"

"No, I don't know what you mean," I said. Fish didn't answer. That wasn't like Fish. Fish always had something to say. Was always running his mouth and would back it up with his hands if he had to.

"Boo, we got two dimes apiece on this game." Ronnie was back to his money. "I ain't got no Benjamins to spare. Let's get something going."

I was working as hard as I could. Waco wasn't kicking my butt, but he was taking me out of the game and I knew I was supposed to be the one collecting the offering.

Fish had a lot of respect for my game. We had made some righteous runs together. Brooklyn, Rucker, Fort Greene, even down to Philly. But he was lying to me about Waco.

I kept thinking about Waco's breath and even found myself trying to get close to his face to see if I was imagining it or something. The dude was strong and he had some game and all that was good, but the cold breath thing still had me going.

When Waco had the ball, he didn't have no big moves. What he had was a steady game and the art of putting the ball soft against the backboard when he was inside. Usually, with two or three guys going up with the ball and two or three trying to stop them, the ball would be bouncing off the rim mostly. But Waco didn't go for the straight-in shot over the rim; he always went for the backboard, and that sucker was steady dropping.

Ronnie was trying to post Frankie, their muscle man, and was getting hacked to death, so he wasn't doing nothing but jawing.

It was looking bad for us. With Waco and Fish keeping our offense on the wings, we were paying for every mistake we made. People along the sidelines was talking, and I imagined them saying how good a game it was, and some were even taking pictures. Probably tourists. But my side was losing, and I hated that crap.

Dudes were already lining up who was going to run next.

I had tried to muscle Waco, and he could give as well as he could take. I had tested his heart, and he hadn't backed off. Now I knew I had to test myself. I had to step up and call my own number.

"Get the ball to me," I said as we huddled. "You dudes 'bound and I'll bring us back."

"Bet!" This from Earl.

I had to say something to Waco. Maybe it was really me I was talking to, but I knew I had to say the words so I wouldn't be backing down on no humble.

"Yo, Flake-O or Waco or whatever your damn name is," I said, looking him dead in the face, "it's my game now."

When he grinned, his face looked like a wound you see in the morgue. Then, for a moment, he looked serious, like he was thinking. Then he leaned forward and said, "I hear you."

With Waco's words came that same freaky cold breath.

I know I can hoop. I know what the ball feels like against the palm of my hand even when I'm laying in bed or walking through the supermarket. I know what it feels like against my palms and going off my fingertips. I know the feeling and I love it. I love it because that's the way it's supposed to be.

I got the ball and took it straight to the hoop. Waco went with me, pushing me farther out from the middle than I wanted to be, than I needed to be, but I still made my move, still went up, still put it up over his outstretched fingers, but it rolled around the rim and missed. Ronnie copped the tap in, but I dug what was happening. Waco had taken up my challenge. He was telling me to bring whatever game I had.

Fish brought the ball down and ran LD into a hellacious pick. He came down the lane and threw up a soft hook that I slapped away. Ronnie got the ball, but Waco slapped it away from him, recovered, and took a dribble. He had dipped his shoulders on the dribble, and I knew he wanted to slam over me.

Street ball. No blood? No foul!

I went up with Waco and brought my body into his as hard as I could. He hung on to the ball, took the impact, and then let it go. Off the backboard, around the rim once, twice, and then drop through. They were two baskets away from the game.

Then it came to me, like one of those times you're not even thinking and your whole body kind of shakes. My grandmother used to say that when that happened, a rabbit had jumped over your grave. That was how the thought came to me. It wasn't about the money, or even the run; for some reason Fish had brought me to Waco. Me and Waco was what this was about.

Earl lost the ball, and they scored again. Ronnie was desperately trying to talk us back into the game.

"I put the money up, and I ain't no charity, dudes," he kept saying. "I ain't no charity."

Ronnie and I hooked up on a give-and-go and he scored, but they only needed one more basket.

Fish was taking the ball out, and Waco came running downcourt. I stopped him with a hand flat against his chest. He stopped and looked toward me. His eyes were so dead-looking I thought he might have been looking at somebody on the street because he wasn't focused on my face at all.

He turned at midcourt and looked toward where Fish had just started his dribble. LD picked Fish up at three-quarter court, but I knew Fish could handle the ball. Waco didn't move until Fish had passed us and we both turned.

Waco ran me into a brush with Marcus and then another with Flyer, but I still stayed with him. The ball went inside, and for a moment, I thought Flyer was going to try the last shot but he didn't even look toward the hoop. Instead he made a bounce pass out to Fish.

"You gotta win by two buckets! You gotta win by two buckets!" Earl was screaming. Keep hope alive.

Fish in the corner with Jamal all over him. He put up a high, arcing shot, which bounced off the rim, off the backboard, into the hot July air, black against the blue of the downtown sky. Then it was me going up, and Ronnie going up, and this incredibly white hand, fingers straining, reaching for the ball, reaching. Me spreading my legs, waiting for Waco to grab the ball and come down, waiting to get all over his white ass, and then seeing him turn his hand and push the ball up as we all came down, watching it hit the backboard as I hit the ground, watching it roll around the rim, watching it fall through. Watching it fall through. Game over. Time to sit down.

"Why don't you hang around?" This from Fish.

"Nah," I said. "Got some things to do."

He shrugged and turned away. No easy Fish chatter. No quick Fish mouth.

I felt a little sick to my stomach and told myself it was from the heat. I took a squat against the fence and took a sip of warm soda as some guys started the usual argument about who was running next.

"Hey, why don't you guys wait around and play it back?" Waco was by my side. I looked up at him. His eyes still looked dark, vacant. The thought of his breath made me feel cold as we stood there in the rising West 4th Street heat. I realized I was looking away from him, but I didn't want to look him in the face.

"You got all my money," I said, trying to force a smile.

"No problem," Waco said. "You can owe me."

"I don't think so," I answered. "I don't think so."

"Fish said they play some hellacious ball in Harlem," he went on. "He said they got guys up there whose whole life is their game. I'd love to play up there."

"I guess he knows what he's talking about," I said, turning away.

Me and Earl left; the rest of the guys hung for another run. On the way home, Earl said he thought we should have won the game, that they had gotten lucky.

I didn't answer Earl. As I hit the uptown A, I was thinking about Waco's remark that for some guys in Harlem, basketball was their whole life. And about him wanting a piece of that action.

NEXT

Charles R. Smith Jr.

"Ay, Water Man, who got next?"

"Oh, no, you ain't getting me in with that mess. Y'all be about to kill a brutha over who running next."

"I'm just saying yo, you been here for a minute, so I figured—"

"You figured wrong, playa. But if you wanna find out, go ask them cats."

"Serious? Yao Ming and Bruce Lee?"

"You asked."

"Mannn, when did THAT happen? Where all the bruthas at?"

"Don't you watch the league, playa? The game done gone *inta-national*."

LAWS OF MOTION

Bruce Brooks

As KaySaan watched the second game, score now 4–3
Skins, he became aware that his head was swivel-
ing with unexpected regularity: left-right, right-left,
left-right . . . *I might as well be watching Ping-Pong,*
he thought, Ping-Pong played by slow amateurs, not
those frantic Asians who stand twenty feet back and
blister the ball so it's a white streak. Yes: the five men
(plus basketball) moving in one direction can be seen
as a spatial and even temporal unit (the serve); then,
after between five and seven seconds, the other five
(plus ball) move the other way at almost exactly the
same speed (the return). The details, to KaySaan,
were not very interesting. Whether one unit spent
its five seconds in the offensive zone combining a
pick, two passes, and a reverse layup or spent its five
seconds doing lots of dribbling before heaving up a

woeful jump shot mattered not to KaySaan as much as the pattern.

Score now 7–5, the team with two white boys ahead. KaySaan heaved a sigh. In about eight minutes — longer if there were more woeful jump shots clanging awry — he would have to tighten his shoes, replace his round metal real-life spectacles with his plastic Sportz Lenz goggles (which could only improve his vision to 20/60, but did anyone ever consider *that* when you missed a four-foot hook shot? One might be six ten, but one still needed to see what one shot at.), and step onto the court.

Someone slapped him above his right elbow. He looked down at the eager face of one of his brothers. "You see that block-out?" said HanNoy, pointing with his chin. "See how that big white thing moved his feet?"

"No," said KaySaan. "I didn't see his feet."

"To get your tall butt into position, you don't just *leeeeean,*" said his brother, nudging him hard — and, one could guess, ineffectively — with his shoulder. "You move your *wheels.* Move your wheels, boy, and your tall-ass self follows."

"Wheels," said KaySaan, looking back at the court with new interest. Yes, the *back-forth* thing worked if you thought of each unit of five as a great wheel, rolling one way, hitting a wall, then rolling the other way. Wheels, five into one. Mildly interesting.

"Two buckets for Skins and we go," said HanNoy.

Approximately three minutes later, they went. KaySaan walked to the middle of the court and stood there as if waiting. In fact, *actually* waiting. CyGonn, his other brother, grabbed his left arm above the elbow and yanked.

"No jump ball out here, fool. Can't you remember for one whole week?"

"I like the jump ball," said KaySaan, getting dragged into one half of the court. "It's interesting. If you wait until you see the ball hang for the tenth of a second — or perhaps an even briefer moment — in which it actually *stops,* then —"

"This isn't about *interesting,* Kay. This is hoops. No money in the game, but you got to still *think.*"

CyGonn pushed him into place, next to the taller white guy from the first two games. The white guy was a few inches less tall than Kay, but the expression on his face — *Stick your hands anywhere near me and I will eat them right off your arms* — added a good foot to him.

"Hi," KaySaan said to the white guy, just to, you know, fill an interlude. "I guess you like basketball."

HanNoy, holding the ball at the foul line, turned and said over his shoulder, "Just stay between him and the hoop. And get your hands up."

Kay raised his arms. Han bounced the ball to a

fidgety black kid, who immediately lofted it to Kay's guy, who spun to his left around Kay and banked in a layup.

"Don't stand there like a streetlight. Get upcourt!"

"Right!" KaySaan trotted to the other end. By the time he got there, Cy was on his heels, dribbling the ball.

"Low! Go low!"

Obedient, Kay crouched. Cy groaned and passed to his friend Tweet, a straight one-handed pass off the dribble quicker than an idea, quicker than a sneeze. But Tweet rushed his right-handed push, and the ball, looking suddenly sort of *stumpy,* with no grace at all, ponged off the front rim. It ponged right to Kay, barely rotating, which was possibly intriguing. But ignoring this rotation business, Kay surprised himself and shot it back up, two-handed (unconsciously imparting, he noted, lots of backspin). The ball crept over the front rim and through the designated hoop.

"Look in your pocket, you find a twenty," said a guy on the other team. Kay started to put his hand—then he got the joke. Jogging back, he told the kid, "You're right. I was lucky. But you know, the chance incidence of—"

The fidgety guy guarded by Han passed once more to Kay's man. Kay jumped to a spot between him and the basket and raised his hands. Instead of eating them, the kid took one step back and jumped and shot. Kay heard the ball pass with a *ching* through the chain net.

"Stick close, fool!"

So it went, back and forth.

KaySaan genuinely tried to concentrate. No: in fact, he *did* concentrate. For example, he counted the number of dribbles each person took, figured an average, and wondered, *but only briefly,* why a person's height was inversely proportional to his urge to pump the ball against the concrete; e.g., the smallest guy on the other team averaged fourteen dribbles every time he possessed the ball, the tall white kid only 1.5. If figuring all of *that* didn't take focus, what did? Trouble was, paying attention did not tell him what to do. His brothers told him what to do, and he appreciated their assistance, but, well, none of his tasks was very interesting, so he could not come to care very much. This was the ninth straight Saturday of giving his best (nine Saturdays *not* spent reading the expensive science magazines at the library or plotting the developing swimming skills of the recently born female walrus at the New York Aquarium or continuing his three-year [so far] project to sketch every gargoyle he could spot in Manhattan), and he had made little progress.

At least he was at last doing what his brothers had been begging him to do since he topped six feet in the sixth grade (*early* in the sixth grade). The twins were three years older than he was but had stood five eleven this spring at graduation. As far back as Kay could remember (pretty far back—he recalled the taste of the infamous cherry-vanilla cake his mom had attempted for his second birthday), Han and Cy had seemed to love basketball above all things. His pops had supported this happy fanaticism. When Kay started zooming up around age eight, all three of them tried to jolly along in him what they believed simply *must* be a profound predilection for the game. I mean, if God gives you the gift of great height, how can He withhold a mania for hoops? What else would He make you a giant *for*?

Through a few years of disbelief becoming frustration becoming resignation, his brothers had never turned mean on him: deep down they could tell he was simply the city's tallest book nerd. His father's disappointment was rougher; the man could never convince himself entirely that in Kay's lack of enthusiasm for basketball against his own passion for it.

It seemed there was a lot of mistaken thinking that could be undone just by the simple gesture of participation. So—with the proviso that he might never be any good—Kay started going with them to the courts. That first Saturday, he was not aware of having contributed anything to what turned out to be a marginal success. The game whizzed and bounced around him. He did not find even an ingress for *thought*. For the last four games of the day, he was commanded simply to stand with his hands up in a particular spot at each end of the court. Twice, driving opponents twisted close, threw up shots, and the ball hit his arms unbidden. *Passive arboreal defense,* he thought.

That first week, they won a few. His brothers were huge in happiness. Their general giddiness included much mild, sardonic gratitude for Kay's willingness. And week after week, they kept asking him back.

He hoped they liked memories, because today this first game was fast running away from them. Kay, who was never certain whether a basket counted one or two (it changed from game to game, did it not?), had lost track of the score, but the trend seemed to be that the other guys scored almost every time they had the ball, while Kay's brothers did not.

Kay found his thinking drawn more and more into the scheme of basketball. For instance: In what ways did the rule of alternating ball-possession establish the rhythm of competition? Did knowing you would get a chance to score as soon as your opponents scored cause an unconscious relaxation of the desire to stop them? Something like, *Oh, well, at least we get our shot now.* If hoops operated the way Ping-Pong or volleyball did — keep serving as long as you win the points—would defense be a more desperate affair, balanced between the need to break the other guys' momentum and the temptation of despair as the juggernaut kept rolling? For three trips down the court, Kay conducted a mental experiment—easy because the rules of the game had not worn grooves in his soul or his brain—in which he banished the idea that a bucket by the bad guys merely opened an opportunity for his own offensive fun. *If they score, we don't get to touch the ball,* he gnawed to himself.

For the first defensive spell, Kay thrust himself much closer to his man, moving his feet as his man dribbled to the right, then to the left to stay thick between the ball and the basket behind. His man, looking a bit peevish, passed to a teammate who missed a long jump shot.

Next time down the court, he pressed even closer even earlier—no sooner had the tall white guy crossed half court than Kay jumped in his face. Very annoyed was the guy, especially when Kay started waving his arms. Nobody passed the ball his way; nobody even looked.

Third time, Kay chest-bumped him, and the guy missed a bounce pass from the point.

Kay concluded that facing no prospect of readily getting the ball indeed made one hungrier for a stop.

He did not get time to cogitate on this, however. Dribbling deliberately upcourt, the guy called Zeke announced, "One more and you tools walk."

Kay looked for interpretation to his brothers. Their faces said it all: no brightness, no tension; they were about to lose.

Something stirred in KaySaan's chest.

Two passes took the ball to a rugged black kid behind Kay. The kid dribbled once, gathered himself, and sprang toward the rim, extending the ball gracefully in his lead hand, unfurling his fingers to let the ball roll, natural as water downhill, through the hoop.

As if watching someone else, Kay took a bound toward the shooter, stretched his arm cleanly over the kid's head from behind, and, with his own equally graceful fingertips, flicked the ball. This lightest of touches was enough: the ball dinked off the rim, Kay gathered it in, and, looking upcourt, flipped a baseball-throw past an unbelieving Cy. Cy ran the ball down and made a layup. Kay was barely aware of himself. The touch! The backspin of the ball as it left the shooter's hand, the tiny mechanisms of his digital tendons following a command his brain hardly knew how to give, the corrective nudge that broke the shot's course! This was, this was — not exactly physics; no, there was obviously some neurology worked in, but, jeez, *this was a new science.* Kay blocked the next three shots his opponents took: two rash ones from within ten feet of the basket, and one telegraphed heave from what he believed his brothers called *downtown.*

At last he was learning something. Some spatial calculus without words, unlike anything else he knew—but, hey, experience was turning into insight *somewhere* deep in there. The littler white guy dribbled off the top of his foot when Kay waved an arm in his direction. Tweet hit a jump shot. Cy and Han stood a bit straighter.

Then Kay's man, responsibility for whom belonged only to the previous incarnation of he who had become KaySaan the Wonder Man, snatched a pass, roared as he rose, and slashed the ball through the hoop with both hands. Game over.

Cy and Han each took one of Kay's elbows and pulled him off the court. He amazed them no less than himself by resisting. "But—" he said. "But—"

"Was cool to see you wake up a little and get big," said Han. "But they beat us."

"But it's getting interesting," Kay said. "See, from the angle of the elbow, you can anticipate the trajectory—"

"Over for now, man."

They reached the sideline. Kay watched another fivesome step onto the court.

He wrenched his arms free. "No!" he said. "I'm starting to get it! I want to—"

"Hey, stick," said a stocky black kid who had walked onto the court. He looked straight at KaySaan; the brothers dropped away. "If you want to, like, keep playing, you can step out with us."

Kay looked. A kid who had gone out, maybe six five, was now slinking toward the sideline, shooting a low look of death at Kay. "What?" Kay said.

"Play like you just played, we get some propers," said the stocky guy. He tossed his chin at the slinking kid.

"He OK with it. He only out here to impress his sister's friend, and he so bad, he won't do that."

KaySaan found his brothers' eyes. "How long before we get back on the court?" he said.

They looked around. A crowd. Ballers. Cy shrugged.

"Two hours, maybe three," he said. He looked at Han, and they nodded. "Do what you do," he said. "We'll be here."

Kay stretched up high, then reached down and pulled up his socks.

"OK," he told the stocky kid. "Let's play."

MY BOYS

Charles R. Smith Jr.

My boys be ballin'
in battle-worn sneaks
wearing attitude like
baggy shorts. My

boys be slight
of frame but
big on game. My

boys be calling shots
before they even
touch the ball. My

boys be speaking
with they hands,
dishin' passes
to the masses. My

boys be soaking
net cords with
jump shots like
summer showers. My

boys be caught
off-guard by
doves floating
outside the cage. My

boys be bouncing
brown spheres
off backboards, bustin'
rusty rims with nasty jams. My

boys be running
and gunning like
they life
depended on it. My

boys be shinin'
like diamonds
under pressure.

MIRA MIRA

Willie Perdomo

I'm standing by the newsstand, texting Margie (again), begging her to come to the Cage. She hits me back and says she has to see because she works on Saturdays. I hate waiting outside of the Cage. I get really anxious being that close to the court and not being able to play, so I stand by the train station and watch people spill out of the West 4th Street exit, hoping Margie is part of the spill.

Word is out uptown that there's going to be scouts looking at ESPN and some of his boys today. Most of these dudes are going off to college. Big D-I schools. They say I can't play with them. Too small. Too much attitude. Out here, though, people will remember. Out here folks have playground memories. People will watch ESPN play, and the stats and the reports and the commentators will say that ESPN is a star, but there'll be someone who was at the Cage and they'll remember how I put it on ESPN. Today, it's going to happen.

"Caesar, you ready?" It's Earl, asking me from inside the Cage.

I walk up to him and say, "Been ready."

"It's me, you, Chester Divine, LD, and we need one more. We need one more to guard their big man, Waco. We need to put a body on him."

"I was thinking about the Chinese dude."

"He's Vietnamese, bro. Get your Asians right."

"I don't care where he's from. The boy got game."

"Nah, let's go for big man over there by the handball court. I've seen him in the chip before. We need someone who'll make them kids think twice about hitting the boards, a bruiser that'll tire them out. Don't worry. Once we start running, they'll know that we don't care if we break something." Earl got a way of talking with his hands. It's like he's conducting an orchestra. After every point he makes, he claps his hands. "We not here to look pretty. Let's really put it on these cats. They got sanitation game; they stink the streets up something nasty, and I heard that college boy you was talking about is here too."

"Who, ESPN?"

"Dude is going to UNC, I heard."

"Well, I guess we'll see then, right? Yo, if you see Margie in the crowd, let me know."

"Keep your mind on the game, man. Damn,

that's why you in the mess you in now. You got no discipline."

"Get outta here with that."

I hate when they start talking that "no discipline" shit. It's not that I don't have discipline. Last year — it's true — I was hanging out with the wrong crowd and I messed up with Margie. I played myself. But I'm not hanging out like that anymore. Took my GED and killed it. Took my test to be a cop, post-office worker, correction officer, all that. Be like Little Eddie. Forty-two years old, dude is about to retire. But it wasn't just the crowd, though. It's that — look, how am I going to think about basketball if I have to take care of my *abuelita,* make sure there's juice in her fridge, make sure she got her meds, make sure the super does work that needs to be done. I'm all she got right now. It's not like she said, "No, I'm not going to take care of him" when the courts were ready to put me in a group home. Grandmoms is all I got. Her and Margie. I don't have to be in college to play basketball. Today I'm just trying to make these cats recognize.

"Caesar!" My uncle Charlie — I call him Tío — yells from the front of Mickey D's, milk shake in hand, asking me if I want one even after I told him like five times to get a bottled water, but he'll come back and say he couldn't find a pump, thinking that it's still 1972 and he's still playing with Spanish Doc and all those cats from East Harlem. Tío is a little off, a little touched, but he has a good heart even though his mind might not be right. Now, if there's someone who would've tore this blacktop up, it would've been Tío, but he got called for duty in Vietnam, and my mother told me he was double *tostado* when he got back. The boy had jumps, though. For real. I see ESPN from the corner of my eye. Always shining, ESPN. I look at him like I'm in such a zone that all I see is his body broken up like pixels through the Cage gate, like he's shattered already. All his gear is fresh: new Airs, clean wristbands, got his goggles, knee pads, and you look into his eyes and know he can't play the whole ninety-two feet. He's one of those half court players. Press him hard enough and he'll sing. He got magazine moves, and he probably never left his heart on the court.

"You ready, *mira mira?*" he asks.

"I got your *mira mira.*"

He walks toward center court like he got a video camera following him.

Man, that girl with the white shorts is a beast. She reminds me of Margie with that slim waist, thick badunka, big, curious eyes walking down Lexington on a summer day. I'm better when she's around. . . . Dude called me "mira mira." You believe that shit?

• • •

ESPN walks up to Earl and asks when the game is gonna start; he's tired of waiting.

"*Oyé, Caesar, limpia el piso con ese pendejo,*" Tío says, taking a sip of his shake.

"Don't talk that *oyé* talk here, *papi.*"

"He'll talk whatever he wants," I say.

"You talk mad brave for someone who can only get as high as these nuts."

"Yeah, OK. Wait till we get on the court."

"*Dejalo que habla, Caesar. Espera que lo cojas en la cancha a ver quien va hablar. Ese que se ríe último, se ríe mejor.*"

Some dude—think his name is Ups—pulls up behind ESPN and says, "Caesar, what's good, bro?" I recognize him from the tournaments at LaGuardia House. He's another one who got a full ride.

"Everything good. Congrats on the ticket, brother," I say.

"Yeah, man, thanks. Down south. ACC."

"Give them some of that LaGuardia House flavor."

I'm not a hater. The next dude's success has nothing to do with me. But don't act new. I know Ups from around the way and he never been one to act new. Not like ESPN. Ups keeps it gully. If he's on the sideline, waiting to get it in, I'm definitely picking him. But today he is my enemy.

"*Papi,* marycon," ESPN says to Tío.

My uncle looks at ESPN with that demonic stare

that my mom says he's famous for. You can call Tío a deadbeat, a drunk, an illiterate, a no-dick, but you can't call him a *maricón*. It doesn't play well with him. Tío gets up and tells ESPN to step around the corner, so he can stitch his mouth shut. ESPN keeps walking, again, like he's the movie of his own life.

Tío. Damn. People think he's crazy because he dresses like a reverend for fun. Thing is, when we see the world standing up, Tío got a way of flipping it so that it's us that's upside down. He could've made a name for himself in the chip. If it wasn't for seeing all those burning bodies and shit . . . I bring him to my games because I know how much he loves basketball. Dude is like a walking way-back-in-the-day video special. He tells story after story about the Spanish Doc, Corky, the Goat, the Destroyer, Helicopter, Pee Wee Kirkland, all those cats; all those cats who were game tight. Some who made it, some who didn't. Tío taught me one thing: the game is lost before the first whistle gets blown. It's like a heavyweight who can whiff defeat from across the ring. When you play ball, you can see the game to the last buzzer. It's like you can hear a door being shut in another part of the world. I hope some of ESPN's coaches are here. I'm gonna take him and turn him into a broomstick, the one with the hard bristles, the kind they use to sweep the curbs. I'm not worried about it. I ain't got no one to impress, nothing to lose. After

this, no basketball camp, no training, I'm just going back
to the block, hopefully chill with Margie and tomorrow—
go to work.

Fish comes over and says, "Yo, Caesar, get it in today."
"Whaddup, Fish. That's the plan."

*Fish is a cool blanco. Met him up in the Jungle. Fish got
heart. You can't sleep on crazy blancos like Fish. They're
down for whatever. I still remember that day when some
dude from Brooklyn was talking all kinds of smack, started
calling Fish "Cracker This" and "Cracker That" and Fish
said, "You know how the Indians had names like Dancing
with Wolves? Well, my name is Dancing with Big-Ass
Bolas!" and Fish put a step on the floor and the next thing
you know he was flying high and what made it worse was
that when he dunked the ball, the ball went bouncing off
of Brooklyn's head.*

"Yes, he was!" Tío is starting up with the who-was-
the-best argument. By this time, he got a group of
people to argue with: one older dude with a *Village
Voice* rolled up like a telescope, another wearing avia-
tor sunglasses (scout), one dude with a Mohawk, and
his girl, a dirty blonde who's smiling and entertained,
her skin all flushed like she just came out of the gym.
    "Hell, no, he wasn't! I don't care what you say.

Magic was better than Bird!" the dude with the *Voice* yells.

This is Tío's way of getting the crowd pumped, so pumped that they're willing to climb trees just to see the game. I've seen moments when a game had to be stopped because some kid started at the foul line, spun a three-sixty, and dunked it. Fold-up chairs came flying onto the court and people in the crowd covered their faces like they witnessed a tragedy and a miracle at the same time.

I walk over to Tío and give him my bag with an extra pair of kicks, a towel, my house keys, my money, and my phone. I check my phone one more time to see if anything came in from Margie and there's nothing but a text from Los saying that he's on the way with some fellas from Lexington. Just to mess with Tío, I throw in, "What about Bill Walton?" and he pinches his nostrils together with his fingers.

Come to think of it, I need a name. "Mira Mira." I like that. Mira Mira, look, blink, oops, too late. Mira Mira, now you see it, now you don't, oops, you ate it. Yeah, Mira Mira, stop, go, oops, sorry. There comes that moment when your heart doesn't pump Kool-Aid anymore. It's like an ice cooler in front of a bodega; the only one who got the key to the lock is the owner.

•   •   •

"Yo, c'mon, they're ready," Earl says.

When you're outside the Cage, you actually feel like an animal waiting to get back in, and once you get back in, you never want to come out. We all meet at half court, give each other polite Obama-'n'-Michelle power daps, and I notice that the sidewalk is getting deeper with bodies. It's lunchtime in the Village and folks are sipping on their Frappuccinos, lemonades, eating their turkey sandwiches, and sneaking incognito sips from a straw out of that afternoon brew in a brown bag. You can even hear some jazz rehearsals sneak out of the Blue Note. The playground hum grows in waves.

By now, my uncle got a crew sitting around him and a few of the fellas from Lexington have just arrived. Los is there. Papú, Davi, Fat Phil too. That's the thing about my dudes from the block. Their sense of timing is dead on.

My crew is here—it's on. All I need is for Margie to come through. Forget that. If she comes, she comes. If not—cool. There's work to be done out here today. Gotta show these dudes that I got game. I'm too short, they say. Too short.

"Game is over when the game is over, fellas. Make them play the whole court!" Tío shouts.

What Tío means is that as soon as the first

inbound pass, we press from one side of the court to the other. Never let up.

"I ain't go no objection," ESPN says. "I got Mira Mira."

"I got LD," says Ups.

"I got the new jack," Waco says.

"Ain't nothing new about me," New Jack says.

"Fellas, bring it in," Earl says.

"I hope you all are ready for this ass-whipping," ESPN says. "It's gonna be some hot peas and butter out here today."

We huddle, and Earl starts with his clap-talk. "OK, look. Ain't no refs out here, ain't no endorsements, ain't no DJs, ain't nothing but us, the ball, and the ground. This is our game." Earl points to the big man and says, "Rick, this is Caesar. Caesar, Rick."

"Whaddup, Rick," I say.

"Big man, put a body on Waco. Tire him out, and we gonna crash those boards like it's a Sweet Sixteen," LD says.

"Got you," Rick says.

"Listen, man, I didn't come from uptown to play just one game. I'm trying to stay out here all day. You heard? The name of the game is press," I say.

"Word," LD says.

"On three," I say, putting my hand out so they can follow. "ALL DAY. One, two, three!"

"ALL DAY!"

The clapping outside the gate starts.

"All day, all day, all day," yells Tío, clapping. "Put it on that fake basketball hero, Caesar! He looks scared!"

The first thing I have to let ESPN know is that I know his weakness. I've seen him play before. Seen him in the Rucker, Gauchos, and at Riverside. He got a good jump shot and knows how to move without the ball, but when he got the rock in his hand, he can't go left.

They get the ball first. ESPN plays the baseline. I get to him right away, and he looks shook. I force him to his left, and the first thing he does is look to pass. Tío once told me to imagine I'm something like a net, a flyswatter, or a sponge when I'm playing defense. Today I'm a glue trap. As soon as he takes the eye off the ball, he's stuck. Sure enough, he takes his eyes off the rock. I tap it out of his hands, grab it, and spin toward our basket.

"Yeah!" LD yells, lifting his right arm to let me know the break is on.

"Go ahead, Caesar! And one, baby!"

"Go, kid! Go, kid!" the *viejo* next to Tío yells.

I pass the ball to LD, who is automatic on filling the lane. We got Waco in a cross fire, and I know that LD is making his way to the board. LD passes back to me and starts his leap to the board. Waco tries to block the shot and LD smashes it, a dunk that leaves the backboard shaking. *Oooohs* travel down 6th Avenue like a local bus.

"That's OK," ESPN says. You can barely hear him, it's so loud on the curb.

Soon as Waco gets out-of-bounds, Rick picks him up. Everybody picks up a man. Waco looks panicked.

"Press!" Tío.

Waco tries to bounce the pass between Rick's legs. It bounces off of Rick's right leg and I grab before it goes out-of-bounds. I spin and pull up for a jumper. *Fwip!* Two.

"Yeah!" LD yells. "Yeah!"

We hold them like that for a few baskets. They can't make the adjustments. Whatever plan they have is totally disrupted. The thing is, everyone on my team is used to running. Running to the store, running to school, running on the courts from sunup to sundown, and back in the day, during those wild Purple City days, some of us used to run from the Boys. It's what we do. That's the way guerrilla wars are won, and if basketball is not guerrilla warfare, I don't know what is.

ESPN gets a few shots off, sinking some three-pointers, but his teammates, even Waco, can't stand the pressure.

"Yo, Caesar, they can't stand the heat, kid!" I hear Papú's voice.

"Word! Show them what Lexington is made of, son!" Davi.

"Go, Caesar!" *That* voice I know. I heard it before. I could hear it in a Times Square New Year's Eve crowd. I look up and it's Margie. Hair pushed back, hoops on her ears, and that cheesy smile. I see her wave, and ESPN spins around me and slams it home.

"C'mon, Caesar, stay up," LD says. "No letup, right? No letup."

"You got that," I say.

ESPN calls time-out because one of his contact lenses fell out. I walk up to the gate and wave Margie over.

Damn, she's looking good as always.

"I got your text, babe," she says.

"Listen, we're almost done with these dudes. We're scraping them. Hang out for a little. Why don't you stick around, hang out with Tío. You know how much he likes you. After we finish, we can go eat some Papaya's."

That's what we used to do whenever I came down here to play. Go eat a couple of Papaya dogs with everything, some papaya or grape juice. That was always the deal. I do something I like: playing ball. We do something she likes, like go to a movie or a poetry slam at the Nuyorican Poets Café.

•   •   •

"I can't. I have to work," she says, pouting her lips as if to say, *I'm sorry.*

"So do I," I say.

"Call me when you get back to Lexington," she says.

"C'mon, Caesar!" LD is waving me over.

"Give me a kiss."

"Caesar," she says, as if to say, *Don't start.*

"C'mon, through the gate." I put my lips through the diamond and stick them out like a fish that has his mouth tied shut by a string.

"Caesar."

"Un beso, ma."

She kisses me, and I can smell the something something *fleur* on her neck.

Tío yells, "Yo, get back in the game! That's how the great heavyweights go down. Love!"

"Took Ali," says one of the old-timers.

"Tyson, too," says Mohawk.

"Let the man play," someone yells.

"Mind your business!" Papú yells.

"C'mon, Mira Mira. Game ain't over yet. You can talk to your pigeon later," ESPN says.

"That's a dove, you fake-ass baller," I say.

It's our ball. Rick passes it to me, and ESPN tries to hem me up. I start talking mad shit in like a crazy whisper. "That's right, it's me, Mira Mira. C'mon, let Mira Mira make you look stupid." I dribble while

I look at him. Going left, going right, then I put it between my legs.

"See, you can never get something that beautiful, something that sweet because you a fake one, and I ain't got time for fake ones. You just look good. C'mon, it's Mira Mira. Oh, watch it, watch it." I see LD about to set a pick at the top of the key. I cross over with a mean first step. ESPN is so caught up in my trash-talking that he doesn't hear Fish yell, "Pick!" And bam! ESPN runs right into LD, and I hear the breath come out of ESPN's mouth when he goes, "Uhhh . . ." The crowd goes, "Ohhhhh . . ." I pull up at the top of the key, and *fwip!* The pill goes through and the net barely moves.

WILD CATS

Charles R. Smith Jr.

12:28 P.M.

Sweat-covered sinew
shines in cage, attracting eyes;
predators stalk prey.

VIRGINS ARE LUCKY

Sharon G. Flake

"There he go."

"Don't let him see me!"

I duck behind my cousin. "Is he looking?" I jump up, look over her shoulders, up and down the court, and then duck back down like she's wide enough to hide me. "Don't introduce me. I can't meet him today."

"What?"

"Act like I didn't come."

"Naw. Naw. You wanted to meet him, and now . . ."

"I told you. My period's on."

She stares at my white shorts. I bought them especially for today, especially for him. I forgot I was gonna have *company*. And none of my friends wear my size, so I had to wear 'em. Now I'm sorry.

We quit talking and watch the court. They're running up and down, slapping the ball, grabbing the ball, losing the ball, moving and sweating and making us sweat, too.

"All those legs," my cousin says, even though she has a boyfriend. "All those fine guys with them wet, sweaty legs—yum." She licks her lips full circle, like buttercream icing is on 'em, then pulls at one of my long curls. "You better meet him while he wants to meet you." She looks around at all the girls and women doing just like us—watching them. Hoping they watching us too.

He dribbles the ball and passes, then smiles at my cousin, who yells his name, and then points to me. A guy from the other team knocks the ball out of his hand and heads in the other direction.

I tell my cousin Ly-nette that it's bad luck to meet a boy when you're on. Her eyes roll, then she points high and low. "See her. And her. And them. They all wanna meet him, but you gonna meet him. So quit it."

I look at her, then I look at him. "OK," I say, thinking about what Ly-nette said yesterday, that a guy like him and a girl like me was meant to be together.

Some of these guys play every girl they meet. Then some like *him* keep to themselves. They come to play, then leave. But when you fine like him, leaving ain't so easy. People follow you, girls mainly, grown women sometimes, and kids and men who ain't interested in your looks but your hands and jump shots and moves. If he was from around here, he'd have a reputation by now. And maybe a baby or two. But he's from way across town. His mother drives him to the court and then stays the whole day. She don't sit in the car waiting, either. She sits in a lawn chair by the fence, knitting, paying bills, and watching the game, and the girls, until he's done.

I hear he goes to an all-boys Catholic school and spends his summers in the country, and not Atlanta, either, but the sure-nuff country where they got chickens and cows and cotton fields too, I bet.

My cousin's fingers slide through my hair. Then she pushes one of my sleeves off my shoulder, just a little. "Show something." She steps back. "They your competition," she says, pointing, "So act like you know."

I stare down at myself. I'm wearing all white. I don't mind saying it: white sure does look good on me. I mean when you put caramel on vanilla ice cream, how can it not look good enough to eat? Only I shoulda picked something else to wear today. Black, maybe.

A guy passing by stops, but his eyes don't. They go up and down me three times.

My cousin is older than I am: nineteen. She's been with the same guy for four years—"So I know

how to get and keep 'em," she says. She asks the dude
if she can help him.

He smiles. "Sure. What's her name?"

She smacks her lips, and holds on to her hips. "I
wasn't asking you that question for real." Her arms go
over my shoulder. "She's sixteen. A baby. A virgin . . ."

I push her. "Don't put my business in the street!"

His smile gets as big as the McDonald's arch
across the street.

"And she's gonna stay that way," she says, walking off with me.

My cousin Ly-nette says being a virgin ain't nothing to be ashamed of. It's just that virgins don't know
how to market themselves. "It's like having a courtside seat at the Lakers game and not wanting nobody
to know you there."

I think if you tell a guy that you're a virgin he's
gonna try his best to make sure you don't stay one.
Ly-nette doesn't see it that way. "It's just a way to
advertise," she says, "not give out free samples."

So she's been advertising me—not with flyers or
nothing, and not to just everybody and anybody. Just
to him, Chester, the guy I'm supposed to meet. This
is what she did—walked up to him one day in the
middle of a game and told him he needed to meet
me. Of course she almost got slapped by one of them
guys. "She's smart, pretty, petite, and a virgin," she
told Chester. "You're gonna like her." Her boyfriend,

Marques, was in that game. I think that's the only reason she didn't get hurt.

My cousin is in sales. "You got a product; you gotta show people how it's different than the other products." Then of course she told him that me being a virgin was not an invitation for him to change my status but just to see how unique I am.

The good thing is that he and I ain't that different. He's a virgin too. He didn't tell Ly-nette that. She found out. She knows somebody who knows somebody who knew him when he was young and that woman called the neighbor up the street from him who talked to a woman at his church whose daughter goes to the school across the street from him.

Basketball players can get any girl they want. And they never keep just one for long because, well, there's all them other cookies out there for them to taste, my cousin likes to say. But Chester's mother makes sure he doesn't taste anything, and she's trying to keep it that way. It's just him and his mother at home. And they do everything together, I hear. Girls and babies are not a part of his mother's plan, people say; a two-hundred-and-forty-million-dollar contract is, or him playing ball for Italy as soon as high school's done. So she holds him as tight as gums hold teeth, and nothing's gonna spoil her plans.

Chester's seventeen and fine. Every girl who sees him wants him. Sometimes after he's done playing, thongs fly. He never stops to pick them up like some of them do. He steps over them like wet tar. So I thought he was gay for a minute. So did my cousin. But Ly-nette got to asking questions, and she watched him like he was free cable TV. She hit him up whenever he was leaving the court, always asking if he wanted to meet me someplace, sometime. Then Wednesday, Marques calls her and says it's on. Chester's mom is outta town on business. "So he's all yours," Ly-nette's been saying.

I walk over to the hole in the fence and watch him play. He jumps and shoots. Everyone claps when he scores. I jump and clap and smile like he's mine already. Then I get to thinking: A boy who's a virgin and plays basketball—how'd that happen? Does his mom go to his away games too? Does he date, ever? Or is he a virgin because he wants to be one, like me?

Ly-nette hasn't stopped yelling since Marques got in the game. "Marques! Get that ball. Yes! Run, baby—make that shot. Yeah! He is so good. The best," she says, hugging me.

Marques's game's not so hot, but even I'm surprised that they don't pick him up for the next game. Ly-nette says he's tired from working a double shift last night. But I know the truth. He just can't play all that well.

"I love that boy," she says once their game is done, and he's walking off the court.

I ask Ly-nette about Chester's status—him being a virgin, I mean. It's one of the reasons I wanted to meet him. Plus it gives us something in common. It'll make me feel like he won't be pressuring me. Besides, a guy who's a virgin has gotta have a lot of discipline and self-control, which means he's probably got his head on straight too, I tell her.

Chester walks in circles, waiting for the next game to start. Him and his boys slap each other five, bump fists, and get ready to do their thing again. "Ly-nette," I say, holding out my hand, "I need to change." I lower my voice. "Get my tampon out of your purse."

Right then, Marques walks up. "That's nasty." He wipes sweat off his forehead. "Guys don't wanna hear that." A whole bottle of water is down his throat and running down his chest in two seconds flat. "Ahhh . . ." Then he's standing behind her, holding her tight and kissing her behind the ears, on the neck and shoulders too. "Chester's gonna quit early. He'll be here in a minute."

Ly-nette faces him, stands on her tippy toes and wiggles her lips. Marques bends down kissing her forehead. When they're done, she opens his hand and kisses his palm, then licks the sweat, just once. "You gotta get the game in you," she always says, "so you remember why they love it almost more than you."

I am not swallowing anybody's sweat. But I would like a boyfriend, a kiss—something. I'm pretty—

guys always tell me that. Only girls like me—virgins—have a hard time getting a guy. Most guys like doors that open fast and easy. The ones they gotta pull on or can't open up at all are just too much trouble for 'em, I guess.

I walk over to McDonald's by myself. I need to take care of my business. I stay awhile, drinking orange soda and eating fries. As soon as I'm back, Marques points Chester's way. "Hey . . . here he comes." Then he tells Ly-nette, "Right after you introduce 'em, we're leaving."

Ly-nette wants to stick around awhile.

"No. They're gonna be fine. What else two virgins gonna do but talk?"

Chester walks over to us. My stomach knots up and my hands shake, so I hold them behind my back.

He's tall and dark brown from the summer sun beating down on him all day long, and wet—from his forehead to his shirt and down to his sneakers. "Hey."

He speaks to Ly-nette and Marques first, then smiles when he looks at me. "I'm Chester." His hand goes out. It's soaked, sweating like everything else on him. "Sorry."

"I'm Irene. Ly-nette's cousin."

Chester and Irene sound like an old, white couple, I think.

"Nice game," Marques says, slapping him five.

Chester's team won. I bet that's why he's still

smiling. He leans against the fence, yelling at someone on the court before he gets back to me. "I'd play in my sleep if I could."

I don't like basketball that much, but I'd never say that to him. I come because of my cousin. She comes because of Marques. Him and Chester talk about the game for a while. Ly-nette asks him how he made those last few shots. I wasn't here, so I don't know what she's talking about. But I notice the girls not far from us. They stare at him and lick their lips a lot. I pull my cousin aside. "Don't leave. I don't know what to say to him."

She's not leaving. She promises.

"Yeah, she is," Marques butts in.

She points. "We'll be over there."

"No. We'll be in my ride, in the air-conditioning, cruising and chilling."

My cousin starts to complain.

He whispers, "She's sixteen. Quit babying her."

And before I can say anything else, they leave.

As soon as my cousin goes, so does my tongue. Ly-nette told me this would happen. "So talk about the game, or golf or anything you saw on CNN," she said. Only as soon as I open my mouth to ask him a question, the fence shakes like the guy on the other side is trying to pull it down.

"We won and you quit? Walk off? Just like that!

Naw . . . that ain't happening," the guy says. He's taller than Chester, maybe six eleven or so. But he don't have Chester's nice muscles or moves when he's on the court.

"Look. I told you: I had something to do." Chester never raises his voice, but another guy from his team does. He's Asian, with blond streaks in his hair, complaining about having to pick up somebody else when nobody's as good as Chester.

"Talk to her some other time," he says, sending the ball into the fence.

I jump back, staring at the missing tooth on the side of his mouth when he comes for the ball. The other guys on his team yell for these two to come on so they can get started. They look like giants, his team. No one is shorter than Chester, who the newspapers say is six eight.

Chester smiles when he looks down at me, asking if I play sports or know his cousin, who has a barbershop near my house. We talk about church — only not too long, because my cousin says that can be a conversation killer. School. Sisters and brothers. Movies. TV. Twittering and videos on YouTube. We talk about all that. But then our conversation dries up fast. He's watching the game again. I'm wiping my forehead and looking up at the sun. He stares at the game like he wants back in. I stare at my feet like I need to be someplace else. The girls not far from us stare too. And whisper.

Some girls don't wait for a guy to make a move. They do like this girl is doing right now; they step up and take over. She's short, tiny. Her eyes are big, and her lashes are thick and long. I like how she's dressed, so I bet he loves it, the hills and the short, tight beige skirt; the light brown hair, real hair, past her shoulders, straight and shiny. And the perfume she's wearing, it's the good stuff, the best—you can tell. "Hey. I saw you play. You're good."

He introduces hisself. And the girl sort of pushes me out the way. Then another girl comes over, and then three more. He looks up the street every once in a while, like maybe he thinks his mother might show up. Then he smiles and gives someone an autograph and forgets I'm here. I try to get into the conversation, but those girls aren't having it.

"You got a girlfriend?" someone asks.

"I'm his girlfriend," one girl says with a laugh.

They are cute. Tall and short, with long hair, short hair, no hair, fake hair. They have on pink or red lip gloss that makes their lips look thicker, juicier, softer. Even those four white girls—the ones standing with the Korean girl—check him out and try to get to him too. They're almost all dressed alike. Their shorts give him a peek at their cheeks, and their chests don't stay inside their tops; they pop out on the sides or just about jump out their bras and halter tops introducing themselves to him. I wonder if any of them are virgins, or if he even cares.

I back up and let them have at him, then I walk away. I'll call my cousin and have her meet me. Then I'll call my girls and hang out with them. Wait till they hear he dumped me even before he dated me.

"Hold up. Take my number."

I turn around to see who Chester's talking to now. He walks up to me, with those girls right behind. Then he leans over and whispers in my ear. I feel my toes get warm. And then it's like I'm a tree — growing ten feet tall right in front of those girls. I say his number over again in my head.

One girl asks him for a kiss on the cheek. He says sure. Only her lips don't stay on his cheek; they find his mouth. And when he finally pulls away, he's breathing hard and looking around like he could use seconds or thirds or fifths even.

"Chester!"

We all back up.

"Dang," he says, wiping his mouth with the back of his hand. "What's she doing here?"

His mother is wearing a gray dress and black heels. But she's moving like she's wearing flats. "Get over here."

Chester whips grown men on that court. But he walks over to his momma with his head down like a little boy afraid he's about to be spanked.

She says it so we'll all hear. "Didn't I say stay away from girls?"

"Yes, Ma'me. Sorry, Ma'me."

"We got it all planned out, you and me. No distractions, right?"

I hear him say yes, but this time he don't sound so sure.

Some of the girls start to complain.

His mother stops. "Venus and Serena. Michael Jackson. LeBron James. What do they all have in common? They kept their eye on the ball—their parents made sure they did too. You're the best around, Chester. Don't get off course." She looks over at us. "Well, I guess he won't be playing *here* on Saturdays anymore. Y'all can't be trusted!"

The girls follow them, throwing numbers his way. Guys inside the Cage jump and yell and pass the ball. A few of the girls stop chasing and cheer them on. "He's almost a man," someone yells. "He not gonna stay underneath your thumb forever."

I guess he likes what she said, 'cause he turns around and smiles, winking too. Those girls go crazy. Everybody says he was winking at them. I think about his number. How I bet they wish they had it too.

Chester and his mom get into their ride, and then

pull into traffic, beeping at a Cadillac his mom almost hits. I walk up the street and pull out my cell to ask my cousin to come and get me. But then I put it away and stand outside of McDonald's for almost an hour, wondering if things woulda been different if I wasn't a virgin, or if things might change for me if I go home and give him a call.

My friend Whitney says that virgins are lucky. They don't have to worry about AIDS or STDs. And they don't have to worry about bad reputations. But all virgins ain't the same, I guess. Some like it the way they are. Others, like him, are maybe stuck that way because they can't do nothing about it. He won't be stuck for long, I figure. His mother better be ready for that.

"Hey. Irene. Get in."

I take my time getting over to the car.

"Hurry up. Traffic's gonna be a mess. That concert is letting out now."

"You know I can't rush. My—"

"Don't say it," Marques says, getting out and opening the door for me. "I don't want to hear no girl stuff."

I sit behind Ly-nette. She asks me how it went. I start to tell her, but then a big one hits and I lie across the backseat holding my belly.

Ly-nette's so excited. She wants to hear everything. I tell her the story, only not the way it really happened. I tell her the story the way it coulda happened, with him kissing me. And me kissing him back.

Ly-nette asks if I lost my mind. "Kissing him ten minutes after you met." She smacks Marques's arm. "I knew I shoulda stayed."

He asks if she's the crazy one. "You wanted her to meet him, didn't you?"

"You pushed my shirtsleeve down. Told me to advertise. Let him know I was a virgin."

Ly-nette's shaking her head, asking if I remember what she told me about sales and advertising. "Don't give away the product. Know your customer. And make your move at the right time — not too fast, not too slow."

I ask for Midol and a swig of Marques's water. Then I tell them both the truth.

"You think he's a virgin?" she asks Marques. "I mean, maybe he . . ."

Marques says he doesn't know him like that and he don't care one way or the other. "But you," he says, looking back at me in the mirror, "I'ma give you your props. Some girls be so happy to get our numbers — they do anything."

Ly-nette starts naming names. "I guess we need to slow your roll," she says. "Find you someone else."

The car stops to let someone pass. I repeat Chester's phone number to myself, but then I see his lips on that girl's mouth, his tongue wiping off her gloss. I wanna be kissed. I want somebody to call me and not just hand off their number to me like a chest pass.

"Do boys like virgins?" I ask. "And not just because they think they can get them . . . you know what I mean."

Marques moans.

"Well, it's not like I really care what he thinks. I'm just wondering, you know?" I sit up, holding on to the back of my cousin's seat. "When I'm twenty, I still plan on being a virgin."

Marques shakes his head. "I don't think he'll make it that long."

Ly-nette starts talking, but Marques's words step all over hers. "I'ma keep it real, Irene. Every dude wants to date a virgin," he says, turning the music down, "and they all want a new ride too. Not to watch it sit, though. But so they can drive it fast, get me?"

That makes me feel worse. "I'll be all by myself forever, then."

He pats my hand. "Maybe. It's your call." He sits through a green light, even though people honk. "But you're particular . . . special. Don't be changing now. Stay that way," he says, pulling off.

Ly-nette gives him a big one on the lips. "I told you he was a keeper," she says.

Marques turns up the music full blast, and starts

singing. It's Ly-nette's favorite song, so she's going at it too. I text my best friends, Whitney and Monique.

met chester. cute . . . fine!!!!! But . . . ☹ . . . talk 2u later.

Ly-nette asks if I want to go to the movies. I go with them a lot, always a third wheel. "No."

Whitney hits me up. *did u get his #? tlk to him yet?*

I type Chester's number into my phone.

Ly-nette says if he wasn't such a jerk, he could go to the movies with us too.

I write him a little something. *hey it's me. what's up?*

I go to hit send, but then I delete the message and sit back and text Whitney and Monique instead. They're both virgins, like me. They always say I'll be the first one to get a boyfriend, or a call from a boy, or maybe even a text. Not today. Not tomorrow, either. But no worries. Like Marques said, I'm particular. Special. Lucky, too, I guess.

EL PROFESOR

Charles R. Smith Jr.

Escuchame,
listen,
school's in session,
sit down and take notes
as I begin the lesson.
Number one—
don't reach,
you reach,
I'll teach
and show you how sweet
I am with the peach.
Mira Mira
my feet
on the concrete,
as I swerve and spin
with my b-ball drumbeat,
pound
pound-pound
pound-pounding the ball
with hypnotic rhythm
bouncing off walls.
Running and gunning

and crossing you too,
I stutter-step and score
as you learn lesson two:
first you see the ball
then you only see my shoe
then you only feel the breeze
as I blow right past you.
Where you at,
what happened,
you see what I did?
Mira Mira my skills,
you ain't ready for me, Kid!

PRACTICE DON'T MAKE PERFECT

Robert Burleigh

1.

"Got it!"

"Whoa, sucker!"

"Not in my house, you don't."

"Pick right."

"Green it, baby."

Shout-outs and grunts merge with crowd calls and sideline chatter.

One pair of eyes watches, yet doesn't watch. In the July heat, a boy squats, his back to the fence, slapping a basketball between his open hands, left-right, left-right.

"Yo, Kid, we up next. Ready?"

The boy nods without looking up. *Readiness is everything.* Isn't that what Geronimo said once? But where is the old man? Ruben's eyes scan the wire fence, crowded with outside eyes looking in through a maze of wire Xs. No Geronimo. He looks to the one area of the Cage where spectators can jam inside, under the far basket. No Geronimo.

Ruben gazes out at the court just as ESPN launches a too-long, next-to-impossible sky hook from the corner that swishes through the chain-link net. The crowd roars, even as the silliness of the shot makes Ruben wince.

But the boy's main attention is focused somewhere else: on Caesar, dribbling upcourt, smooth Caesar, dribbling with the confident showboat style that Ruben knows so well. All too well . . .

Saturday, three months ago: in the Cage. One-on-one with Caesar. The score rising: 2, 4, 6, 8, 10—to 2. Caesar's wide gotcha grin. Mocking and careless as he bounces and weaves to the hoop, leaving the boy flailing and stumbling. Ruben's awkward attempts to drive. Shame rising in his throat.

"Enough school for you, Kid?" That Saturday, his lip bleeding, and Caesar's sneer. "Come back when you're ready for prime time. If ever."

Ruben glances up as the tide of the game flows past him. He watches as Caesar backs inside, spins, drops a short jumper, then points a mocking finger at ESPN's lazy attempt to block.

•   •   •

That day again. Ruben turning, walking away, wanting to hide. Then hopelessly glancing at Geronimo in his battered canvas chair. The old man's usual station, beneath and behind the backboard. Geronimo. Always there. Watching. Steel-eyed. Silent. Smiling. Is he laughing at me, too? Does the boy dare ask? No way. No. Yes. What the hell. Yes.

"Help make me the best."

"They all say that. You don't mean it."

"Try me."

"They come and they go. You don't have the stay-with."

"Try me."

"You won't last two days."

"Try me."

Geronimo, wondering at this strangely intense boy-man. Athletic, yes, but raw, unformed, one more round-trip rider on basketball's Dream Express. For a long time saying nothing, then —

"Tomorrow morning — six sharp. Bring a ball — if you mean it and if you have the guts."

"Try me." *Ruben, walking off beneath a hail of mocking laughter coming from Caesar's direction . . .*

Still squatting, Ruben begins to bounce the ball between his legs, three inches off the ground, his wrist vibrating to the *tat-tat-tat*, nothing touching but ball and fingertips.

No palm, Kid, fingertips. Geronimo's hard-edged voice, coming from somewhere deep inside the boy's head. Geronimo. Where did that name come from? Was it the red bandana headband over the old man's twisting gray hair? His intense, dark eyes?

And where do nicknames come from, anyway? They arrive, and then they're yours forever, like a scar. Ruben hates his: Kid. Dumb. Young-sounding. He's sixteen in a month. So what?

The crowd noise bubbles up. For a moment, Ruben bristles at the oohs and aahs: sounds like hundreds of voices spilling from the bright-colored uniforms, loud shirts, and garish hats. What are they all doing here, anyway? Isn't this *his* Cage? Isn't this the same Cage where, day after day, morning after early morning, he alone — and Geronimo — broke the quiet with the echo of a single basketball hitting the pavement and one man's insistent voice?

Late April. Behind them, only the occasional dog-walker and sometimes the wavelike whish of passing cars. Ruben leans against the fence, waiting. The ball pinned to his hip by his dangling arm. The old man in his faded canvas chair, squinting as if seeing something far off, speaking slowly.

"There was this famous violinist, see, who had all the chops. He goes to a teacher. And get this. He asks the teacher to start him again, from the beginning, from zero,

from zilch, from nothing! How to curl your hand, how to finger, how to breathe, how to become the music itself."

Then, pausing before gazing sideways and up at Ruben: "That's how it's got to be, Kid. Nothing less. Let's roll."

So another morning begins.

Blind Man
Ruben at the end line. Geronimo at half court. Ruben dribbling toward him, looking up and ahead as Geronimo flashes a rapidly changing number of fingers. Ruben calling out the number: three, five, two . . .

Grenade
Ruben, dancing just beyond the three line. Geronimo, under the basket, flinging the outlet pass. Ruben firing without pause.

Touches
Ruben leaping, tapping the ball lightly against the backboard. Tapping, twenty-five off his right foot, twenty-five left. Then both. Putting the last tap in.

Geronimo's voice, staccato as the steady thump of the ball, punctuating the stillness:

Jab and Attack
"Don't precook anything. Keep possible to the last moment."

Crossover, Juke, and Shoot
"Eyes on the rim, not on the ball in the air."

Figure Eight
"No showtime. Dribbling's supposed take you some-where."

Hops
"The court's a stage, and you're the director."

When Ruben starts to laze, to drift—the old broken record returning: "The great ones never practice, Kid. They always play."

Time. You're streaming sweat. Here. Wipe off with this. Keep it. It's yours.

Ruben feels in his hip pocket for the bandana. Why keep this piece of—? But interrupted by a sudden flurry of claps and screams, he blinks and looks up. Someone has just canned a long trey. Joyous fists stab the air. Caesar's team has taken the lead. *Good,* Ruben thinks. *That's how I want it. We'll see.*

He looks down to the far basket, where a few of his teammates are shooting each time the game races the other way. There is Gene the Machine with his old-fashioned one-hand set shot, Ronnie the Bull, Baby Z.

He lets the ball drop and thump lightly into his hands. The feel of it! The invisible thread!

There are days when everything he sees or senses becomes a piece of the game. When he sidesteps across a busy street corner, he slips inside. When he zigzags down subway steps, he bounces off bodies. When he stands upright in the front car of a rocking train, he stays on his feet and highs to the waiting rim. Did anyone ever love the game more? Well . . .

The old man laughing. His open laugh. "An itinerant philosopher — that's what I am, Kid, a loser who loves this game. A drifter. Halfway from and halfway to: today the Big Apple, tomorrow — who knows?"

Ruben, back to the wall, letting his long legs stretch out across the diner's leather booth while sipping a Coke through a straw.

Geronimo pointing at Ruben's half-filled glass on the table. "Havlicek didn't even drink Coke, to say nothing of beer, his first ten years with the Celtics."

Ruben saying nothing, but later, when Geronimo looks away to call for the check, the boy pushes his unfinished glass aside.

A dark-skinned young man wearing thick glasses dribbles a basketball past the diner window. Glancing up, Geronimo waves. He turns back to Ruben, eyebrows raised exaggeratedly, like a clown.

"Peepers Wilson—he's at the Cage every day, and know what? He never gets better."

Ruben laughing. "How's that?"

"Easy. He's a living example of the fact that practice don't make perfect. Only perfect practice does that."

Practice don't make perfect. Ruben delights in the old man's way of turning things on their head. He wants more.

"Who's the MVP in the Cage?"

"Says here it's that dead-eyed white boy."

"Hunh?"

"Don't look surprised. It's 'cause he gets his team the ball and he doesn't want it back. These days, that's as rare as a dodo bird. Think Dennis Rodman. A nut case maybe, but he's got a ring for each finger."

Ruben again. "Who's overrated?"

"No contest. ESPN. Ask me why. Because he makes some lucky, half-ass shot now and then and can't stop from trying it again and again. There's an expression for jerks like that: 'Good enough to lose.'"

Tidbits tumble out, wiggy shit that bounces around in Ruben's brain for days.

Geronimo, waving for more coffee, forking more eggs, goes on.

"You have to learn everything, Kid—and forget it. Don't keep what you know in your head. Keep it in your kneecap. Your game is you; it shows who the hell you really are: you're soft, you're scared, you're me-me-me, you're 50 percent, you're plain stupid, whatever — it's all there in your game, plain as day, and you can't escape it."

They sit for a moment, the nearby chatter mixing with the distant clatter of dishes. Ruben rolling his paper napkin into a tight ball, flipping it into the air, and catching it coming down.

"I'm ready now, Geronimo. I am. I want Caesar again. Head-to-head, one-on-one."

Geronimo, looking across the table and slowly stirring his cold coffee with a fork. "Patience, Kid. A pinch of it's worth a bushel of brains. Guy I knew in Chicago used to say, 'You ain't home till the invisible laws of the body meet the invisible laws of the game.' Get it? Philosophers call it pure form."

The old man snorts and high-fives the boy. Then, pointing to the big clock above the counter: "Meanwhile, don't drop your day job. You'll be late for school."

Ruben checks the score with someone standing near him. With three to go, it's Caesar up by two. He begins to focus. He watches how Caesar backs into the paint from the right side, how Caesar dribbles slightly higher with his left hand, how Caesar transitions too quickly when the other team shoots.

His skin prickles with a kind of odd intensity. "It's

a game of inches. Know where your man wants to go, and get there first. Be so 'there,' you make him want to give up."

He looks around once more. No one is looking. No one cares. No one knows. And the one person he once thought was there is gone.

"Halfway from and halfway to, Kid: today the Big Apple, tomorrow . . ." It had sounded so cool to him then, one more sign of Geronimo's magic.

Gone for a week now. For good? Probably. Ruben feels like a tiny speck in a vast sea of faces and bodies, like an insignificant mote in a sky of endless blue. Kid. Kid. Was that then? Now?

His hand accidentally touches the bandana scrunched in his pocket. He yanks it out, almost angrily.

Slowly, he wipes his already damp forehead. Will it fit? He starts to twist it around his head in a thin circle. But no. Not that way. His own way. He smooths out the bandana and one-folds it point to point. He lays it lightly on his head, takes the two dangling corners and, tightening, ties a small, hard knot at the back of his neck. Didn't Geronimo say the bandana was *his* now? So—prove it. Make it yours!

An even louder roar goes up. Game.

Baby Z is standing beside him now, shaking his shoulder.

"Yo, Kid. You stylin' with that red rag? We're up. Ready?"

"Ready," is all Ruben says, staring straight ahead.

2.

A Saturday pick-up game on a hot and hazy morning. A Saturday pick-up game — ten players battling for nothing but one more win in an endless and instantly forgotten scroll of victories and defeats. A Saturday pick-up game, like thousands of others before it and still to come.

But inside this game, another game is playing out — with only two players. Caesar, alert and serious now, a slight frown between his eyebrows, eyes Ruben as the boy dribbles, backpedaling to the far side before blasting down the baseline. A half step late, Caesar follows, but walled off by the rim itself, can only watch as Ruben floats under and beyond for a reverse layup: 4–3.

Who is this? A game that began with cool and confident trash talk ("Schooltime again, Kid?") becomes a game for real. Ruben, at the point, glimpses Caesar out of the corner of his eye. His swagger gone? And something else. Respect?

At 8 all, a quick crossover leaves Caesar clutching air. Ruben drives the lane, but jammed by two defenders, flips a behind-the-back pass to Geno in the corner, who lofts a rainbow that drops through the chains with just the faintest *ting*: up one. . . .

10–10: game time.

Watching. Waiting. Remembering. At the exact moment the dribble leaves Caesar's left hand, Ruben pounces — and taps the ball into the clear.

Now there is only Ruben, a garble of screaming voices, the ball before him, and open space. He streaks past half court, across the three circle, and at the free-throw line explodes with one long stride up and up. For a single, split-second, slow-motion moment, the boy rises like a dolphin breaking the surface of still water.

High. Higher.

His arm wheels back over his head. The ball feels small in his grip. The hand comes down. Take that! Clango-bango!

Ruben plunges into the fence behind the backboard, bounces off the loose mesh, and spins to see —

The basketball? Where is it? The ball, catching the rear of the iron and caroming off, sails out and away. At half court, an amazed Caesar hauls it in like an outfield fly. Then he turns around, smiling, and lopes to the opposite basket for the easy final shot.

Ruben slaps the fence with his open hand.

Players pound backs, high-fiving, wiping their faces, clutching fence wires to keep from dropping.

Ruben is still, feeling the energy wash up all around him. Caesar nods as he walks past with his water bottle.

Something makes Ruben turn to the spot where Geronimo sat on his folding chair.

He slams the fence again. Stupid loser! Blew it! It was there for the taking. Should have just laid it in. Should have, should have . . .

"Remember, Kid, nothing recedes like success."

Suddenly Ruben's anger and irritation are swallowed by a laugh that comes from deeper down. That wisecracking old fart! He was always one step ahead of—

"Hey!" Togo and Ronnie the Bull come up and slap at him, pushing playfully at his shoulders, dancing imitation-like from one foot to the other. "You got hops, K-man, you got hops!"

"Yo," says Baby Z, tossing the ball to him. "How's about you in the game after next? We short *one.*"

Ruben tugs at the bandana on his head, pulling it down tighter, then looks up, smiling and dribbling with one hand.

Th-thump.

Th-thump.

"Yeah," he says. "What else we here for?"

THE FIRE INSIDE

Charles R. Smith Jr.

3:03 P.M.

It ain't about hype
or how high you rise;
game recognize game
by the fire
in your eyes.

HE'S GOTTA HAVE IT

Rita Williams-Garcia

Forget being like Michael Jordan. I wanna be like
Spike. Who wants to be the actor when you can move
the actors around the board like knights and rooks?
It's the filmmaker's world, and the spectators stand
in line to buy a ticket to watch, be wowed, and talk
about what you did.

Over a thousand hopefuls apply to NYU Under-
graduate Film and TV every year, but I'll be one of the
few to get in. I've got my essay, all the paperwork, the
fee. The only thing left is to shoot this documentary,
then send it all to admissions.

Documentaries are the way to go. I've seen every
doc Spike's made. *The Original Kings of Comedy.*
4 Little Girls. When the Levees Broke. Kobe Doin' Work.
And more. I've screened them all here, at the IFC,
soaking up Lee's technique. In a few years, everyone
will be watching my film here at film lovers' paradise.

For now I go guerrilla with my old Canon digital, and there's no better place in the West Village to go guerrilla than in the—

My pocket buzzes. I take out my phone.

Where U at? I got next.

I text back a quick, *I'm there,* and reach for my backpack, rising from my seat. "'Scuse me. 'Scuse me." I push past knees and grumbling in a row of Spike lovers and haters.

Last Saturday I hopped the train down to West 4th Street and met this guy, another senior. He saw me shooting three lovelies in short shorts on the handball court with my Canon; I saw him posing after hitting a three. He wanted a highlight reel, and I needed a subject for my film. We struck a deal.

Around here, you say "ESPN" and everyone knows you mean Eddie Newcastle. That's a funny dude, except he doesn't know he's funny. I tell myself, it's about the gig, not the actor. Doesn't Spike deal with difficult actors on every set? I'm up for it. I'm a filmmaker. With film footage, some editing, and a back story, I can turn ESPN into the baller his mouth and profiling say he is. It's all about the filmmaker, not the actor. By the time I finish shooting and editing his high-profiling goofy self, I'll transform him into that clutch shooter the scouts look for. Now, that's some magic. But I can pull it off.

My pants pocket buzzes, but I let it go. The Cage

is directly opposite the theater. It's not like I have to travel. Just cross 6th Avenue and I'm there. I step out of the dark theater with my Canon in hand so I can come out shooting.

You can't miss ESPN. His head is shiny from full-mask goggles and gleaming from a white headband that matches his wristbands. Goofy. I aim from across the street, lining him up while I wait for the light to change. He sees me, starts animating, "Where you been?" with arms outstretched, palms open like that white marble Jesus on the Brazilian mountaintop. Isn't that what they called Ray Allen's character in *He Got Game*? Jesus? I shake my head. Ray Allen, ESPN is not. I gesture back to say, *Put your arms down, Jesus. I got you. I got you.*

The light changes. As I cross, I look down into the canyon of glass and brick Wall Street buildings where 6th begins. An army of yellow cabs stand docked at the red light, set to charge up the avenue. I stop. I gotta have this shot.

"Hey! Hey!" ESPN shouts. "Whatcha doing, man? Over here. Shoot this way."

Actors don't yell cut. That's my call. I ignore him and stand firm on a manhole cover.

The light changes and the yellows advance up 6th, heading straight at me. It's a game of chicken between the cabs and me, and I'm shaking. The cabs honk, swerve; the drivers yell at me. But I gotta have that footage more than I want to live. The last cab whooshes past, and I run across the street, laughing. "Got it! Got it!" I only wish I had someone from class to shoot me shooting ESPN running the Cage. That would have been cool. A "making of" the documentary like Spike does.

I meet him at the fence instead of going around the Cage to get inside.

"We have a deal," he says.

It's hard to take him seriously when his face is coated in Plexiglas, but I stifle the smirk. It's gonna be a long day. "Dude. Hold it together. I'm here. I'm ready."

"Well, act like it. This is my highlight reel."

"You need to calm down. Next game hasn't even started," I say. "Chill while I grab some flavor for the setup. You know. Get the street vibe. The Village vibe. And when the game starts, I'll be on you, and it'll be all you."

"That's what I wanna hear."

I go to work. I shoot the train station elevator as it opens to grab a crowd coming out of the subway. That's my angle: the Cage as a magnet pulling all kinds of watchers, ballers, and regulars. The Mecca. First I'll show the cabs. The crowds. The buses. From uptown, downtown, and crosstown, all rushing to the Mecca. All hail the Cage.

Now the people. I get the schooly-old black dude in his purple turban, long purple tunic, gold beads. I get his maroon Pumas and the Puma gym bag slung over his shoulder. He's straight out of Bethlehem. One of the Wise Men coming to worship. Then I pan the spectators, the bodies lined up, two men deep, clinging to the outer frame of the Cage. I pull in close on black, brown, tan, yellow, white, fingers hooked through chain link. Then mouths instead of eyes. The Cage is tight. The crowd is hungry, wanting to be on the inside, running and gunning. Suits and messengers, all "used-to-bes," playing through the players. All hail the Cage.

And then there's the lovelies, whose nail-tipped fingers also grip the chain-link fence. I grab those long-spined cheetahs in minis and shorts staking out the prey. I forget about ESPN, although he's there in the background, going, "This is my film. My film." But those summertime calves and thighs are too lovely to miss. Six-inch heels talking to concrete. *Look-a-here, look-a-look-a-here.* The Canon loves the lovelies.

"Hey, man. We gonna do this or what?"

I click the pause button. *Do actors tell Spike?*

"Flavor, man. Remember? Like I said, when the game starts up, I'll be on you. OK? All you."

"Top-ten player of the day," he says, shooting and making an imaginary outside shot.

He steps away in time for me to grab this head full of honey-brown locks bouncing my way. The face flashes a cheesy lip-glossed grin my way. I'm not the only one scoping. I guess that's what the lovelies aim for. To stop play inside the Cage for a quick holler. A few guys on the inside oblige, and sure enough, that's all she wants. I take aim. Girls love being shot. No such thing as a girl who doesn't. I call out, "Hey, Lovely. Over here." She swings her head to me, all teeth and lips, proving my point.

I want her to speak, but she doesn't. She just keeps walking, so I call out, "*¿No habla inglés?*" She won't turn around and give me that close-up. One more try in my best fake Boricua, "*¡Mira, mira, 'oni!*" All girls wanna talk to the camera. Canon loves the lovelies, and the lovelies love the Canon.

But then some dude in the Cage turns, looks my way. Says, "What?" like De Niro in Scorsese's *Taxi Driver* film. Like, *Are you talking to me? Are you talking to me?*

All I said was "*Mira, mira,*" but he acts like I'm calling him out and he's waiting. I stand with my Canon. He stands with the ball. It's like Gary Cooper staring down guns in *High Noon*. So I hit RECORD and shoot. The Puerto Rican De Niro turns away.

ESPN's now hot because I shot some other dude inside the Cage. All I can see are those goggles . . . the admissions panel screening my short, checking out the shiny alien, and promptly tossing my reel — *swish* — into the "see ya" pile.

I make a wardrobe call.

"Lose the goggles, E. Looks bad."

He shakes his head. His slick, shiny head. "I paid good money at Niketown. The goggles stay." Actors, man.

The baby of the bunch, a skinny kid with a faded red rag on his head, yells over, "Prime Time!"

Eddie eats up the respect from the kid. He soaks it up and tightens the band on his goggles instead of removing them.

I pull in close on Red Rag and catch the hunger. Note to ESPN: Enjoy the respect. Today it's "Prime Time." Next week same kid'll pull the plug on you man-to-man.

I shoot the Shirts huddling while the Skins still work it out. Both baskets in the main court and the third basket on the side have been taken over by practice shooters.

I pass the next few minutes shooting Fat Man selling his water on the side, another guy selling crates of schooly-old LPs, tape cassettes, and CDs, and Drip-Drip-Artist who, like her paintings, is covered from jacket to shoes to hair in drippy pastel paint.

A ponytail guy around my age leans against the Cage, hugging his ball. Like Red Rag, he's got the hunger, so I get close. All I have to say is, "What's up?" and he starts talking about flying over from France to play, and standing on the outside. Got his ball and everything and afraid to enter the Cage. I don't ask if I can shoot him. I hit RECORD and let him talk. Everyone wants to tell their story. So I get his hunger and fear. Nice.

I shoot ESPN trotting down the lane for an easy two off the backboard. Overshoots.

"Hey. Hey. Not that," he shouts, spotting me. "Only top-ten plays."

I ignore him.

This schooly-old Latino wearing a collar like a priest jumps in front of my Canon. "*Oyé. You making a movie,*" Papi Loco says.

I say, "A film."

"What's this film's about?" His scrutiny is fake. He wants to be in my short. He wants to talk.

"A baller," I say.

"Baller? Which one? Caesar? *¿Mi sobrino?*"

I point to ESPN.

Both laughter and disgust fly from his mouth. "That's no baller. Not that dude. Film my nephew. He's the real deal. Like me, back in the day."

"You ran the Cage?"

He is pure animation. A storyteller to the masses. Suddenly the priest collar makes sense.

"*Oyé,* Fellini."

I laugh. "Get it right, Papi. Spike Lee, not Fellini."

Papi Loco doesn't care. "See these lips?" he says. "*Beso el cielo cada vez.*" He purses his lips and smacks a long wet one into the air. "And I didn't need no hundred-dollar sneaks to kiss the sky and dunk that ball." That's aimed at ESPN, and I'm loving it. Schooly-old versus Niketown.

"You want to hear stories? Stories about real ballers from back in the day? I got stories for you, Fellini. Back when the Spanish Doc, the Goat, Pee Wee Kirkland, guys like that ran the Cage. Back when me and Geronimo used to hop on the blacktop, when it was a blacktop."

Why not? Let the priest confess his story. Bring the flavor with his old guy conjugation: I used to be . . . I coulda been . . . but now I am a spectator.

He tells me his name, Charlie, and I mentally ditch the "Papi Loco" even though he still calls me Fellini. It's OK. The admissions panel will love Charlie. That old tiger got stripes.

"Tío, what's going on?" It's the Mira Mira, *Are you looking at me?* dude.

They pass some rapid Spanish back and forth. The tone Charlie raps says, it's cool. Still, Mira Mira peers into me with no trust, but I don't care. Charlie waves him off, conjugating cool: "It's cool, Caesar. I'm cool. He's cool." Mira Mira gives me another De Niro glare and gets back to his practice shots.

Mira Mira is faking that De Niro glare hard. He knows he wanna be the subject of the film. He knows he wanna be immortalized.

So, I do like Spike did in 4 *Little Girls*. I don't milk emotion from Charlie by asking how he felt back in the day. I just let him talk. The genius of filmmaking is finding the heart, the story, in all that footage. The actor doesn't make the film. It's all about the filmmaker.

Finally. The game starts up again. The Asian twins rise from the cement curb only for Waco, the Great White Shaq, to tell them to sit down. "Other dudes waiting," he says. His word is law around here.

The Skins back Waco up, and the Shirts leave the twins hanging. Skins still need a man on the court, since the other ball-handling white boy's gotta leave. I make sure I grab the two white boys passing more than a handshake between them before one slides.

Waco looks over the bench. I film the ballers waiting for next with their backs to me. French kid sits at the far end. He's there, but he's not the Kobe sub Waco's searching for.

Waco points to a dude in prison cornrows wearing a schooly-old Scottie Pippen Bulls jersey. The dude rises like a giant unfolding himself, but he's not all that tall. Just broad and square.

I turn to get ESPN sinking one from the half court. Finally something to save the reel. But that's when Waco says, "Skins," and the dude tears off his shirt and oh! That's no Kobe. That's a girl in a black bra. A girl!

I shout out, "Girl! Girl! Do it again! Do it again!" She hears me but won't turn around. So Mira Mira taps her shoulder, says, "'Nique," and points to me and my Canon.

She spits on the blacktop and turns her back.

What?

I'm kicking myself. I coulda faked that ESPN shot. I can't fake the shot where she takes off her jersey and transforms from "he" to "she." And she won't turn around. I am kicking, kicking, kicking myself.

I enter the Cage.

The guy who she sat next to gets up and snags the jersey off the blacktop. At least I get that. Him snagging the jersey and giving it a good shake. He takes his time folding it but keeps his eyes on her while she's running and gunning.

ESPN shouts, "On me, on me," and lets his man sweep past him. No surprise there.

I focus on the game. Try to live up to my end of the deal. ESPN makes a few nice outside shots. He gets a few *oohs,* but he's allergic to the paint. The crowd knows he won't play defense.

Then 'Nique serves up a no-look reverse layup without stopping to watch the ball spiral and drop straight down through the net. She draws some crowd cheer, but doesn't stop to bask in the nastiness of her shot. She's already down the court. Back to D.

Now I'm on her. All her. She's keeping up with

the run, although no one's passing to her. I don't think she cares. She stays on her man, tries to make something happen. Go for a steal, her arms long and ripped.

The guy she's guarding tries to send her a message. I can't blame him. Who wants a girl guarding him? Red Rag and Mira Mira are all hands, open, free, shouting, "Open! Here!" but the guy wants to keep it. He lowers his head and bulls into her chest. Stays there, no refs to save her. He just goes for her cushies, pressing with his head and shoulder, waiting for her to "girl" on him. Cry or slap him.

I stay tight on her face. That's not a crying face. I see it in her eyes, and I pull back to get the full body, knowing something's up. *Stay on her. Stay on her.* My man doesn't realize her wingspan is ridiculous. She reaches in, sucks up the ball in her massive hand, spins strong-side for the steal, and passes to Waco for the stuff. Crowd is still oohing while 'Nique trots backward, ready on defense.

I can't even fake interest in ESPN. I make the recasting call and cut ESPN altogether. A couple of three-pointers won't wow the admissions panel, but this girl will. I gotta have that shot. I gotta have that girl to save my reel and get me in.

Oh! She catches the wrong side of a size 14E and some shoulders and goes down. She pushes up off the blacktop, dusts off, and runs. And I got that. Canon loves her heart. Her skills, but damn! Why does she do it? Take that punishment? Keep running and gunning?

I squat next to the guy who grabbed her jersey. "Hey."

He nods.

"Look. I'm doing this film."

"A movie?"

"Documentary," I tell him. "For school."

He nods, says, "Oh," like he knows what I'm saying but he doesn't have a clue.

"I'm shooting your girl."

He smiles at that but stares straight at her, following her, coast to coast. I put the camera on him. "'Nique, right? Monique?"

"Dominique."

"Sweet," I say. "How long she's been coming to the Cage?"

He shrugs. "Long time. She rings me, says, 'Scotty, swing by. Let's go shoot some hoops.'" He reddens. "She shoots. I watch." He licks his bottom lip, meaning he doesn't want to look crusty for his close-up. If Scotty wants to be in it, maybe she'll want to, too.

"They don't always let her play," he says. "Depends who's there. Big white dude's cool."

I get a nice Stockton-to-Malone pass between 'Nique and Waco. I start to feel good about my reel and break the rule of Spike. I ask, "How do you feel watching her get pushed around like that? They punish her, man."

Another shrug. I press.

"Can't be easy watching your girl get banged up by all those guys. You're her man, right?"

He says, "We tight."

"But you don't like it when that happens. They jam her, man."

My face and the camera lens become one thing to him. He talks to us both about her. That this is all she wants. The Cage is the only place where it counts. I get a few minutes of him talking, but it all comes down to the one line I'll use: "Dominique's gotta ball."

"Thanks, man," I say, and I mean it. "All I need is a shot of Dominique sitting next to you, waiting to get next, then rising up slowly and pulling off her Bulls jersey." I sound like a director. A filmmaker.

He stares at me blankly. Then he laughs with his whole body.

It's like Mira Mira staring me down. I don't get it. So I ask, "What's funny?"

Now only his eyes laugh at me. "Dude. She won't do that. Pose for you. I mean, you can get her running the Cage, but play-acting? Naw, man. Not 'Nique."

So I shoot. Wait. Watch the game. Shoot as much of Dominique as I can get.

Finally. Game. Scotty holds out her water bottle

as she slogs our way. She's been through the war. It's in her eyes. She doesn't look happy about me shooting her, but she'll want this reel.

I shoot her grabbing the bottle.

"You're in my space. Move."

I step aside. "It's cool, it's cool," I say.

ESPN is beefing in the background, but I tune him out. Even though she hasn't softened, I keep talking and shooting while she guzzles.

"You're the star of my—"

She throws the bottle at Scotty. He misses and it hits the ground. "Zat on? Get that out my face."

"But you're the subject—"

"Get that the helloutmyface 'fore I yoke you." Her left hand balls into knuckles and veins. Whatever I missed from far away, I have close up: rage.

She's no yellow cab swerving to miss me. She's ready to "yoke me" and my camera. She frames me up tight. There's nothing to ask her. Tell her. I'm tasting my insides, and it's not good. I put down my Canon and back away from her.

ESPN stays on my tail and in my ear about his highlights. I "yeah-yeah" him, but I don't look back. I'm out the Cage, hopping over to the subway elevator, glad to get out unyoked with my Canon in one piece. My heart slams my chest floor on the ride uptown. I'm praying I got something. I'm praying hard. Actors, man. Can't shoot a film without them.

BACK IN THE DAY

Charles R. Smith Jr.

4:18 P.M.
You remember Goat from way back?

Do I remember Goat! Shoulda been called Eagle the way he flew. You ever see his double dunk?

AWWWW, yeah. Where he took the ball, dunked it, and—

Caught it before it landed and dunked it again!

Ain't never seen nothing like that!

Right? What about Helicopter?

Come on, now, who you talking to? Of course I remember Helicopter! Used to put a dollar on top of the backboard—

Then snatch it off and—

Leave change!

Yoooo, that was my MAN back in the day!
What about Pee Wee?

Shoooooot! I seen Pee Wee put in work all over
the city.

Right, right? Remember that one time he put it on
Nate the Skate?

ONE time? Mannnn, he put it on Nate MANY
times. Uptown, downtown, Brooklyn —

Yeah, Pee Wee put it on a lot of cats back in the
day. But not like Joe Hammond.

Awwww now, there you go! Startin' something. You
HAD to bring up the Destroyer!

Ay, that was my MAIN MAN.

You remember that time he dropped fifty in a
game?

He ALWAYS dropped at LEAST fifty in a game.
Right, right.

I remember this one time up in Harlem, at
Rucker, right, Joe's team was playing Dr. J's team for
the championship, only Joe didn't show up till the
second half. It wasn't no thang, though, 'cause they
won after the Destroyer dropped fifty on the good
doctor himself.

How you know?

Mannnnn, I was there, yo.
Yeah, right!

Ay, if I'm lyin', I'm dyin'!

HEAD GAME

Joseph Bruchac

Drop a basketball off a girder four hundred feet above the street. How high you think it'll bounce? Bet none of them know. But I do.

I cough, turn my head, pull out one of the tissues I have stuffed into the hard hat I'm holding in my left hand. Spit, check it. For a change, it's just the usual New York City pollution, yellowish brown.

I lean against the outside of the Cage. Been leaning here so long and hard against the woven steel links that when I straighten up, there's a pattern pressed into my forehead. Shape of a diamond. Its sides the four sacred directions. An hour Billy and me been here. I was here earlier this morning, checking it all out. Plus I been here long before that. But this is Billy's virgin visit, and his jaw is still bouncing off the pavement every time some high flyer does a semi-Jordan flying dunk.

Me, I may be somewhat impressed, but I am remaining impassive. Wearing my stoic Indian look. Pop brought me here first time when I was ten. Three summers before the fall that killed him. Pop was one of the Mohawk ironworkers who built the WTC—whose Star Wars ruins I was in town a few years back to help take down—he brought me down here. All the way from Brooklyn, little Kahnawake, to see the sights of lower Manhattan. Pop wore his hard hat the whole time, the one with a war eagle painted on it. Letting people know who he was. First the roof of the Twin Towers, where Pop's bonnet gained us admission and he showed me where his name was scratched into the highest piece of steel. Then the American Indian Museum, followed by the Statue of Liberty, for everybody but Indians. Then the highest point of it all for me, the Cage. And one individual in particular.

"See that guy." Pop nodding his head toward a lanky light-skinned man in loose clothes sporting an Afro the size of a hot-air balloon. "That's the greatest basketball player who ever lived." Then Pop laughed. "And don't he know it? Son, that is Joe Hammond."

Present day. And I'm wondering how many of the under-thirties out there banging inside, elbows flying, even know who Joe Hammond was. Can they see his ghost standing over there by that bench watching? Or maybe it's not his ghost. Maybe it's the man himself.

Heard a rumor he was still among the living. But if so, how come I'm the only one seems to see him? Unlike everybody else here, including the dudes out on the court.

I wonder if any of those high-fly ballers were among the kids who saw what I saw right here a decade ago to this very day. How Joe Hammond strolled out to midcourt, almost absentmindedly. The game stopped; everybody stood aside. And when he held out his right hand, he didn't even have to say, "Ball." They just handed it to him. Then he stepped forward a few feet and began making two-handed shots, one after the other. Every one a swish. Fifty in a row. Other players just shagging the ball, passing it back to him. It was a red-hot day, sun beating down, but there wasn't a drop of perspiration on his forehead. He stopped after that first fifty buckets, bounced the ball once, turned, walked a few paces toward the other basket, and did it again. Another fifty in a row. Nothing but net.

Then he flipped the ball back to the last guy who'd fed it to him.

"Play on," he said, and wandered off the court in our direction. He seemed totally unaware of anyone around him. However, as he walked past us, he looked up, took in Pop's hard hat and then his face.

"Chief?" Hammond said.

"Hi, Joe," Pop replied, holding up his hand for a

high five that made its way into an Indian handshake. It surprised me how Hammond was easy with that, knew the way Skins shake hands. Which I am not about to describe, and if you don't know it, too bad.

"My boy," Pop said, indicating me with a turn of his head and a thrust of his chin. (Indians don't point with a finger unless they are being rude or challenging someone.)

"He got game?" Joe asked. Neither Pop nor I answered him. We just kept quiet. Answer enough. Hammond's smile got broader, and he held out his big right hand to tap me in the middle of my forehead with his thumb.

"It's a head game, my man," he said. "You remember that?"

I still remember. Which is why I left early this morning to come back later. Why I have been watching for so long, picking up their moves, analyzing their games, and thinking how to get in—for as long as I can last. Even just one basket. But I need to do it in a way that'll get 'em thinking, give me the little edge I need. Play with their heads.

Meanwhile, though there are no Joe Hammonds, no Goats, not even no Anthony Masons, or Smush Parkers, I've been enjoying watching. It's not tournament time here at the Cage, no orange and white jerseys. No MVPs. Just Shirts and Skins. But there's plenty of talent here, enough to field a five that could kick the butt of any team in the Sweet Sixteen on a given day. Interesting cast of characters, too. Ranging from the stereotype street-ball nut to the downright sinister. More on that later.

Meanwhile the one I'm liking best here is the Taino—which is how I always think of Puerto Ricans; can't help but see the Indian first, I guess. My own weird sort of racial profiling. One of the shorter dudes on the court, but managing to bully the bigger guys by playing roadrunner to their coyote. Darting in and out like a bat shagging flies in the twilight, stealing the ball when the kid in goggles tries to dribble around him, taking it downcourt to a layup as smooth and cool as a drop of rain running down a window.

Caesar, he's the Taino guy. Thought at first his moniker was Mirror. Then realized that was just some name another half-ass was taunting him with. Until my island-brown brother showed him up. Caesar's good. I like the way he looks over now and then and nods to the older man who's watching his bag. Tío, who's been having arguments with everybody—not mean words, though. Playing, teasing—like some of my own uncles back at the Rez do. It's plain that T knows hoops, was a player here in his younger days. Probably the one who's taught Caesar those moves. Only one he can't get by with them is the dude on the other team, the sinister one.

Yup, sinister. That one there, Waco. White as a knight of the KKK and a lefty, at that. He was here for the first game back at nine A.M. Midafternoon and he's still here and still not breaking a sweat. Smooth, but scarily so.

I've been reading those cold, empty eyes of his. He wasn't playing for money in that first game. Which was sort of an anomaly here. Playing a money game.

You don't come to the Cage for the bucks, but the baskets, the adrenaline-pumping excitement of the texture of the ball in your hands, hearing it thump in rhythm with your heart against the court, then letting it and your breath go in a shot that arcs up and goes through. Seems to me that's the real reward.

Like it was for Joe Hammond. Pop told me how the LA Lakers heard about this legendary player, brought their whole team east to check him out, invited him to practice with them. They ended up so awed by his ability that they offered him a fifty-thousand-dollar contract. Mucho dinero, back before ten-million-dollar players.

"Joe just laughed," Pop said. "Said fifty bills was chump change. He had more walking-around money in his pocket any weekend. No way was he leaving the neighborhood. He was pulling down a quarter mil a year hustling pool, playing dice. But he didn't use hoops to make money. That would have been like selling his soul. So Joe never went to LA."

Yeah, there are some who go on from here to college ball, even on to the pros. Some here in the hopes of getting filmed for a commercial or a documentary. There's always more than one camera scoping the action at the Cage on any sunny summer day. Plenty of players trying to ham it up for the lens, hoping for their five minutes of Warhol.

But for most, just stepping into the Cage is enough. If it wasn't, there's no way the one named Dominique would be daring it, the only girl playing today. Check that big girl ignoring the taunts, the hard fouls. Takes in a no-look layup back over her right shoulder, not even turning to see if it goes in. She's already downcourt on D, brushing past Caesar, who's standing there shaking his head, sorry she's on Waco's team and not his.

The big white shark nods as she reaches in and strips the ball from the big guy who tries to body-block her and ends up stumbling over his own feet. She dribbles twice, then passes it out to Waco. His gaze downcourt pauses at me, leaning against the Cage. His eyes try to bore into my head. I don't make eye contact, just hold the same blank expression. Yeah, he wants me.

Makes me think of something I read. How a game like basketball was first played a thousand years ago in Mexico in a stone court with a rubber ball and vertical stone hoops on the walls. Serious stuff. Sometimes the members of the losing team were decapitated. Sometimes the winners. Willing sacrifices, supposedly, to the gods who loved the game so much they wanted the best players with them down in Xibalba, the underworld. Talk about cutthroat recruiting. Talk about a real head game!

Maybe Waco thinks he's one of those old blood-hungry deities. Eh? Hell, maybe he is one. I believe anything is possible here in New York City. And I'm already seeing ghosts. But whoever and whatever he is, Waco is as hungry as some sort of psychic vampire. Wants me like he wanted that one kid who was in the first game I watched. Boo, they called him. He was so shook by what he saw in the big white guy's depthless gaze that he lost his game, froze up even though he seemed to be a better player. Then, after he and his buddy paid up, he split the scene entirely. Leaving part of himself behind. A little of his soul taken. Waco looking an inch taller, got some of what he was here for.

"Game's almost over," Billy said, his hand on my shoulder. "You going to try to get in the next one?"

Billy Laughing, my cuz on Mom's side. "Come on," he says, "dare ya!"

Four little words. Yup. Same ones that made me consider wire-walking the high cables of the big bridge from Cornwall Island when I was twelve. But the three other words that led to me actually doing it are the next ones he speaks in the same tone as back then.

"Bet ya won't."

You ever do something that someone else wants you to do, even though you know that they're pushing your buttons? Like the last time Billy pulled his five-word manipulation on me. I was sitting having lunch from my bucket, my feet hanging contentedly over fifty stories of empty space, our crew just done with hanging the iron except for that one long girder hanging from the giant crane in front of us. Same size crane as that one that tipped over a few seasons back and took out an entire half block in Brooklyn.

I'd just cleared my throat for the tenth time and hawked one up that was about the same size and color as a ripe plum when Billy came up and sat next to me. He pulled a big shopping bag into his lap. Looked at me. Said nothing. Neither did I. Minutes passed. I finished the last of my ham sandwiches.

I knew what Billy wanted me to do: ask him what's in the bag. So I sighed inwardly and did it.

"What's in the bag, cuz?"

But he didn't answer. Instead, he looked over at that girder.

"Is that wide enough to dribble a basketball on?"

Crap, I thought. "Maybe," I said.

"Could you do it?"

"Maybe," I said. Then I sighed, outwardly this

time, and said the words I knew he was waiting for. "But I don't have a basketball."

"No problem." He reached into the bag and pulled it out. "An authentic signed LaVonne James."

"It's LeBron James, doofus," I said, snatching the pill from his hands and then staring in disbelief at the signature.

"Like I said"—Billy grinned—"LaVonne James. What do you expect from a ball made in India and bought off the back of a truck for $11.95?"

By now, as usually happens when Billy starts something, we'd attracted a crowd. The rest of our crew had drifted over.

"BB's gonna dribble this basketball on that girder."

"No way."

"That's crazy."

"It's impossible."

"Suicidal."

And which of the previous statements did I totally agree with? And what was next said by my cuz? Yup.

"Dare ya. Bet ya won't."

Yup. It was possible to dribble a basketball on a girder. Twenty times, in fact, before my coughing fit and the sudden gust of wind, the tip of the boom, and my own decision not to follow its descent led to me grabbing the cable and watching the L. James knockoff diving like a red-tailed hawk toward the blocked-off avenue empty of pedestrians and then . . .

Bounce high enough to clear the seven-story warehouse across the street?

Explode into countless fragments of synthetic subcontinent rubber?

Impale itself on a piece of rebar sticking up from the unfinished frame below?

Use your imagination.

Something I always do. I've read more books than your average Mohawk ironworker, may even make it to college someday. I know from the fatigue I felt this morning that I won't be able to hang iron much longer. But I won't be on any college team. They only take players with enough strength left to play at least a quarter. Not someone with the lungs of a sixty-year-old coal worker. Not a tall Skin who may look good but is guaranteed to gas out spitting blood halfway through a suicide drill.

Courtesy of the air around the WTC—that invisible toxic cloud that all of us breathed in every day as we worked, the cops, the rescue workers, the firemen, the construction crews, including us Mohawk guys who volunteered. All of us without respirators. A whole crew of us come down from Akwesasne and Kahnawake the day after the planes hit. Thought we could save lives, but when we realized there was no one left buried to dig out alive, we still probably saved some. Our uncles and fathers had put up those towers. So we knew the safest way to take down the wreckage that might have killed less experienced workers than we were.

Game's over. There's a few guys taking practice shots before the next five step up to take on Waco's team. He's staring hard at me, wanting me. Doesn't know how much I understand. That I've already been sacrificed.

Billy is still looking at me. "Bet ya won't," he repeats.

Yup. He said the magic words. Plus I've got my idea about what to do. I take off my shirt. If I'm on any team, it has to be Skins, right? I hand it and my bucket to Billy. Then I turn to the bandanaed kid standing next to me. The one who has been staring at me on and off. A hard hat with a swooping hawk on it and a classic Mohawk profile attracts attention like that sometimes. Nod at the kid. Played some intense ball and missed a slam on his last play four games ago, did better two games after that but his team lost and most of them drifted off. Not him, though. Unlike me, he is holding a basketball.

I jerk my head toward the court. "Take a shot or two with your ball?" I ask. First words since I been here. "Feed you a few after that?"

"Yeah," he says, his face lighting up.

As we walk onto the court Waco steps up, leans close, his breath cold on my cheek.

"What you got, Cochise?" he whispers.

"Not much," I say. I pause at half court, take a deep breath — but not so deep it makes me cough — launch an easy left-handed sky hook so high the ball looks like an orange pebble at the height of its arc. Comes down hard, fast, and true.

Swish.

I look over and nod to the ghost by the bench and the stocky figure who's just joined him — wearing a hard hat with an eagle painted on it.

"That one's for you guys," I whisper. "Next one's for me."

24/7

Charles R. Smith Jr.

Eat.

Ball.

Drink.

Ball.

Sleep.

Ball.

Think.

Ball.

Work.

Ball.

Play.

Ball.

Joy.

Ball.

Pain.

Ball.

Life.

Ball.

Love.

Ball.

I.

Ball.

Be.

Ball.

JUST SHANE

Adam Rapp

You think you know me, but you don't. You see me on the M9 bus or maybe the D train and you're like, that bowlegged skinny white dude is stoopid — why do he got one sock up and one sock down and that's not how you s'posed to wear a baseball hat and why is his shorts so crazy long?

What you don't know is that I'm a lot smarter than you think. Just ask Hazel or the Milkman or Mrs. Honeybuns. Just ask my brother, Waco, who's a straight-up legend at West 4th.

Mrs. Honeybuns's real name is Helen Karlin, but I call her Mrs. Honeybuns 'cause whenever I come to walk her dog, she leaves me a honeybun sweet roll and a glass of orange juice. She's old as hell — like seventy-something — and she lives in this fancy building on East 84th Street with like gold elevators in the lobby and shit. Her dog — this little-ass Norfolk terrier called Tiny Dancer — likes to piss on ten-speed bikes and parking meters. He's got human hair, and when the dude who grooms him comes by, he don't cut it with scissors; he plucks that shit like it's some eyebrows.

After I walk Tiny Dancer, I take the Six train down to the East Village and walk the Milkman's Rottweiler — Mr. Douglas Fairbanks Alaska — and then I take the 9th Street bus across town to go walk the Ryans' dog. It's my favorite part of the job 'cause I get to see Hazel, who lives with her moms on Perry Street.

Hazel goes to this fancy-ass school up by Mrs. Honeybuns's crib called the Chapin School. She has to wear this plaid skirt that seriously messes with my nervous system. If Hazel is home, she'll usually walk her dog with me. They got a puggle, which is a mix between a pug and a beagle, and they named him Derek after Derek Jeter. I always look forward to walking Derek even though something is seriously wrong with his ass, like his shit comes out green a lot — green with mad mystery chunks — 'cause he eats all this crazy stuff he's not s'posed to. Once he ate a wallet and once he ate an unbreakable comb and once he ate some suntan lotion. After we walk Derek, sometimes Hazel will come sit with me in this little garden on the corner of 6th Avenue and Greenwich. They got crazy flowers in that garden. It smells mad aromatic, like we on a island in the middle of the ocean. We usually sit on this one bench and talk.

I'll be like, "How come they don't let dudes in your school?"

She'll say, "Because those are the rules?"

"But why they got a rule like that?"

"Because boys upset your concentration."

I'll say, "But in real life, boys is everywhere. It's not realistic."

Hazel will say, "It's more for the parents than us. It makes them feel safer."

And I'll be like, "They got male teachers in that place?"

"A few, yeah."

"Why do they let *them* in?"

"Because they're adults and they know how to handle themselves around a bunch of boy-crazy girls."

Then I'll look at her out the corner of my eye and go, "Are *you* boy-crazy?"

And she'll smile a little — she's got these dimples in her cheeks that are mad cute — and she'll say, "Maybe a little."

Then I'll say something smooth like, "They should let *me* go to that school."

And she'll say, "The skirt would look pretty funny on you, Shane."

Hazel's got red hair — like it's so red it almost makes a noise when you look at it — and she's mad tall like almost six feet, and I think I might kill someone if I ever caught them messing with her. Her moms is a TV actress and her picture gets put in a lot of magazines. She's on that one show where all the doctors is doing all the nurses. Hazel's moms is the only female doctor and they got her doing this Puerto Rican dude called Nacho who drives a ambulance. Mrs. Ryan is always at this place in Long Island City, Queens, called SilverCup Studios.

Hazel's pops died when she was a little kid. There's this picture of him on their piano and he looks like a spy in a movie. A spy or like he would be really good at throwing a knife at a fugitive.

Hazel thinks I'm sixteen like her 'cause that's what I told her moms back in June when she interviewed me about the job. The Milkman told Mrs. Ryan about me, and this dude from West 4th called Sleepy Jack told the Milkman I would walk his dog 'cause he knew the Milkman needed help 'cause he lives in a wheelchair. When I first came to town, Sleepy Jack was always looking out for me. I met him at West 4th. He would buy me hamburgers and let me use his MetroCard.

During the job interview, Mrs. Ryan said, "You're sixteen, right?"

Her hair is black, and according to that picture on the piano, so was Mr. Ryan's. I don't know how Hazel's hair came out red. Genetics is a trip.

I was like, "I just turned sixteen three days ago."

Mrs. Ryan musta liked me 'cause she went, "Happy birthday. You got the job. Four o'clock every day."

Then she gave me a set of keys and that was that.

I stay in Bay Ridge, which is way out in Crooklyn. To get there, you gotta take the D train to 62nd Street. I live there with my brother, Waco. Waco's real name is Larry but even I don't call him that. Waco ain't really my brother but I tell people he is and he don't deny it. He's like six three and skinny but he's strong the way dogs is strong, and he'll dunk on you without thinking about it. And he'll throw it on you with the left and cross you up and break your ankle before he do it, too. Sometimes he'll break both ankles. He could've played in college — all these D-II schools was looking at him — but his SAT scores was mad low so he joined the army instead.

After he got back from Iraq he didn't wanna do nothing but play ball, so that's all he do now. He's at West 4th every day — rain or shine, all day long — and even though he's been there every day this summer, he don't never get tan. It's crazy. It's like the sun don't know he's there or some shit.

The reason I live with him is 'cause once after he was done playing, I followed him into the West 4th subway station. This was back in May. I jumped the turnstile and sat across from him on the D train and just stared at him. He was eating some McDonald's and he could see I was mad fiending for some so he gave me half his Big Mac.

He was like, "You're that kid Sleepy Jack's always talking to."

I nodded.

His voice was mad deep.

He said, "You watch us play every day."

I nodded again. I couldn't believe he was talking to me.

He was like, "You don't got nothing better to do than watch a bunch of derelicts play ball?"

I went, "What's a derelict?" but he didn't answer.

After a minute he went, "What's your name?'

"Shane."

"Shane what?"

"Just Shane."

He was like, "Aren't you in school?"

I said, "Ain't no school in the summer."

Then he studied me for a second and went, "Is that backpack all you got?"

I nodded.

"You homeless?"

"No," I said.

"Yes, you are," he said.

I was like, "So?"

And he was like, "So you don't have to lie about it."

The Big Mac tasted so good it made my arms mad tingle.

The train stopped for a second and he said, "How do you know Sleepy Jack?"

I was like, "I just know him. He's tryin' to help me get a job."

"Doing what?"

"Walkin' dogs."

He said, "You like dogs?"

I went, "Dogs is better than people."

Then he asked me where I was from and I was like, "New Haven, Connecticut."

Then he asked me why I was homeless and I told him about how I came back to the crib one night and how my moms and her boyfriend—this big West Indian dude called Lennox—was gone and how everything was gone in the apartment too and how I waited around for a few days to see if they was coming back but they never did and how I snuck on the Metro-North train and how I been in New York ever since.

He was like, "You know where they went?"

I said, "No."

He asked me how old I was and I told him I was fourteen even though I was thirteen. But I turnt fourteen on June 20th—I'm Gemini like Kanye West—so it wasn't really a lie.

Then he gave me the rest of his French fries and said, "You don't have any relatives you can stay with?"

I just shook my head and ate the fries. My stomach was going bananas.

Then he asked me if I played ball.

"Not like you," I told him.

The truth is I played on my seventh-grade team back in New Haven but I was the sixth man. I only averaged four points a game. I got a mad good handle, but I can't shoot for shit past fifteen feet.

We didn't say nothing for a while. The train came up from underground, and it was starting to get dark. The other people in our car looked like they'd been on the D train for like forever.

When we was walking to his place on 65th Street, I asked him what all his tattoos was for.

"Stupid stuff," he said.

I went, "Was you in a gang?"

He said, "Yeah. It's called the United States Army."

I was like, "Is that where you learned how to jump so high?"

But he didn't answer me. He was walking all slow and relaxed, but I had to practically run to keep up. That's how he moves on the court too. He goes way faster than you think he going. He's suddenly by you like he *thought* himself past you. Like he got superpowers and shit.

When we got to his crib, he told me I could stay in the other room as long as I cleaned the bathroom twice a week and didn't mess with his stuff. Then he gave me a bunch of his shorts to wear and a few T-shirts too. They're mad huge, but I don't care—it's become my new style.

Like I said, it was May then. It's July now and I got my own money now so I can buy my own shit. Waco gave me his Houston Astros baseball hat, so I wear that too.

In general Waco's pretty quiet. That time on the D train was the most he's ever talked to me.

He does mad push-up and leg exercises to keep his hops tight. He also listens to this crazy-ass rock music, mostly to this band called Liars. The dude in that band shouts a lot. I think he's from England or Germany or someplace foreign.

Waco pays his rent with army money he gets from getting shot in Iraq. He caught a bullet in the kidney and got sent home and now he gets a monthly check. He don't got the Internet. He don't even got a cell phone.

Once I asked him why and he went, "I get tired of people knowing where I am."

I was like, "But what if some girl's mad looking for you?"

He said, "She'd know where to find me."

Which is true 'cause she'd just have to go over to West 4th.

He mostly uses his army money to buy basketball kicks. He also sends a little each month to some lady in Galveston, Texas, called Nancy Fox. I think she might be his moms, but I couldn't tell you for sure.

Once I looked in Waco's room when he was in the bathroom and I saw that he's got mad books. He keeps them stacked on the floor all neat and shit. He's got like a hundred books; I ain't lying. The one he was reading was called *The Things They Carried* by this dude Tim O'Brien. I have to admit that title makes me curious 'cause I imagine all these little kids carrying shit, like car parts and stuff from their cribs like televisions and microwave ovens and toasters and DVD players. I see like a thousand kids and they don't know where they're going but they're hanging on to all that stuff like they'll die if they drop it.

I stay in the room closest to the street. The garbage trucks get mad loud, but I'm used to it. It's better than sleeping in Washington Square Park under those nasty-ass chess tables.

Waco didn't used to make me pay rent, but now that I got my own business, I give him a hundred a month. I still clean the bathroom twice a week, too.

Earlier me and Hazel took Derek over to West 4th to watch Waco play. It was mad hot out, like a hundred-something degrees, but they was balling anyway. The air was so thick, it was like medicine in your mouth. They usually play Shirts and Skins, but the dudes on the court was all Skins and they was mad sweating, too. All the fanatics was hanging on to the Cage like they was getting ready to die, like they wasn't gonna make it up 6th Avenue and holding on to the fence was gonna give them more power or some shit.

Derek was smiling and mad panting. I never saw his tongue get so long.

Hazel was like, "Which one's your brother?"

I pointed at Waco, who was running back on D. He was checking this old skinny black dude they call Methadone Joe 'cause he used to go get his methadone dose and spit it into some other junkie's mouth on the Bowery for ten bones. Then he'd use the money to go score a cheap bag on Avenue C. Methadone Joe's clean now and he's like forty-something years old but he can straight-up play and he'll lock you up on D so bad you'll wish you stayed home.

Hazel said, "You and Waco don't look alike."

I was like, "Yes, we do. Our eyes."

She looked at my eyes and went, "His are darker."

I went, "Mines is dark too."

"Your eyes are green, Shane. . . . I wish I had green eyes."

I was like, "You got fine eyes."

She went, "I'm a redhead with blue eyes. What a cliché."

Then I finally told her what I wanted to say to her for weeks. I was like, "You're mad beautiful, Hazel."

She kind of blushed and pretended she was

looking down at Derek and went, "You probably say that to all the ladies."

I was like, "No, I don't."

Then Hazel bended down and petted Derek for a minute. When she stood up, she went, "How old's your brother?"

I said, "I don't know. Like twenty-something. He fought in the war."

"In Iraq?"

I told Hazel how he got shot in the kidney and how he got a medal for valor but how he keeps it in this little box in his room and don't never show nobody.

She said, "Where are your parents?"

I was like, "Our moms is down in Texas."

"What part?"

"Galveston."

"Do you ever see her?"

I went, "Sometimes we do. We send her money."

Then Hazel said, "Does your brother have a job?"

I told her how all he do is play ball and listen to Liars. I told her how he don't have the Internet or a cell phone.

She went, "Is he OK?"

I was like, "He's straight. He's just real quiet."

"Maybe he should talk to someone."

I said, "Like who?"

"Like a therapist."

I went, "Waco ain't gonna speak to no therapist."

"My mom sees one. It's really helped her deal with my dad."

I was like, "He died, right?"

Hazel nodded, and her eyes got big and sleepy. They were so blue, they made my chest ache. Even though her face was mad sweating, she looked pretty. I wanted to touch her hair, but I didn't.

Instead I asked her how her pops died, and she was like, "He killed himself."

I was like, "With a gun?"

And she went, "With pills."

I didn't say nothing after that.

We watched the game for a minute. Waco caught a tip dunk over this tough Puerto Rican dude called Caesar. The fanatics lit up and shook the Cage and Derek barked his little-ass puggle bark and some shorty in a Yankees hat filmed the whole thing on her iPhone and was showing her moms. When Waco dunks on you, he don't never talk smack. He just runs back on D with this dead look on his face. His eyes go black and it's like he knew he was gonna do it, like he could tell the future and shit.

I think he killed people in Iraq and it did something to his head. Once I asked him about it. We was in the living room eating tacos. The TV was on with the sound off. The news was on, and they was show-ing all these little Iraqi kids running from a army tank. Those kids looked dirty as hell, and I couldn't figure out where their parents was. All the buildings was mad rubbly. Some Iraqi dudes came out of an alley and started throwing rocks at the tank. Rocks and Coca-Cola bottles. It wasn't even fair.

I went, "Did you kill anyone over there?"

But he didn't answer. He just looked at me all dead-like and said, "Eat your taco, Shane."

At West 4th, Hazel was holding on to the fence with her right hand now. You could see how she bit her nails down to nothing. I never saw her biting them, but you could tell it was a habit.

She went, "So the summer's flying by."

I was like, "I'm hip."

"School's gonna start before we know it."

I nodded.

I wondered if we would still hang out in the garden. If Mrs. Ryan would still need me to walk Derek.

Hazel said, "You going to Fort Hamilton?"

I was like, "Yeah."

"Sometimes I wish I could go to a public school."

I was like, "You goin' back to that fancy one?"

"Yep," she said. "Just ordered my new skirt."

"Was it expensive?"

She said, "I don't know. Ingrid paid for it."

I was like, "You call your moms by her first name?"

She went, "Not in front of her."

The heat was making sweat run down my face and in my eyes. They was mad burning.

I couldn't stand lying to Hazel, so I told her the truth.

I was like, "Can I tell you something?"

She was like, "Uh-oh. What?"

"I ain't really in high school yet."

She was like, "You're not?"

I shook my head and pulled the bill of my hat down over my face.

She pushed it back up and went, "Are you like in junior high?"

All I could do was nod.

"Really, Shane?"

I said, "I'm going into the eighth grade."

I felt mad stupid.

I went, "I didn't mean to lie to your moms. I needed a job."

Then Hazel let go of the fence and was like, "Don't worry—I won't tell her."

"Cool," I said.

On the court, Waco grabbed a board and handed the rock to this Dominican dude with crazy dreads called Judgment.

I said, "I told you the truth 'cause I like you."

Hazel was like, "I like you too, Shane."

I said, "On God?"

She was like, "You believe in God?"

I was like, "I don't know. Not really. It's just an expression."

She said, "On God, then."

I went, "You like, *like* like me or you like, like me as a friend?"

She said, "Both."

Then I went, "Word."

And she said it too. She was like, "Word."

Then I took a deep breath and said, "Maybe we could meet up for real sometime."

She smiled and said, "Meet up for real and do what?"

I said, "I don't know. Go see a movie. Do somethin' romantic-like."

She went, "Something romantic-like, huh?"

Her dimples was mad dimpling.

I said, "I might be younger than you, but I got my own business."

Then she looked at me for like a whole minute. She was still smiling. "OK, Shane," she said. "You're on."

On the court, Caesar started talking smack.

He turnt to the crowd and was like, "See what happens if he try dunkin' on me again."

Then on the very next play, Judgment stole the ball from this herky-jerky white point guard with a headband they call Chris Cringle. Judgment threw an oop to Waco, and he caught another dunk right on Caesar's head. The crowd went bananas. Even

Hazel got excited. Judgment gave Waco a pound while they was running back on D. He was so amped, his dreads was bouncing like a monster.

Then Caesar walked right up to Waco and busted him in the face. Waco didn't see it coming, and he went to a knee. The whole place went quiet, and all you could hear was traffic going by. When Waco stood back up, Caesar was right up in his grill, trying to get him to fight. But Waco just stood there, all calm and collected-like. He didn't even blink; he just stared back at Caesar. Then Caesar bitch-slapped him and called him a ho but Waco just kept standing there.

Caesar was like, "You just gonna stand there?" Then to the crowd he went, "Kid don't never go home."

Judgment was like, "Chill, Caesar."

Then to Waco, Caesar said, "Don't you got a fuckin' life, B?"

Then someone in the crowd went, "You're the one who needs to get a life, you big bully!"

It was some old white lady with a cane. She was mad angry.

Then Caesar went, "Punk-ass bitch think he hard, dunkin' on niggas. He ain't shit."

Waco went, "Let's just play," and then Methadone Joe and this little black dude they call Squeaky finally pulled Caesar away and they checked the ball and finished the game.

Waco's team won by four. He could've dunked another one — he went baseline and was mad airborne, but he laid it in with the left. His hand was like a foot over the rim and everyone knew he could've banged it.

Even Hazel knew it.

She went, "He could've easily dunked that."

I nodded and smiled.

Waco's mouth was mad bleeding, but he just kept playing through it like pain ain't nothing but a penny you keep in your pocket.

REPRESENT

Charles R. Smith Jr.

"What's going on? Are they about to fight?"

"Ahhh, a buncha nothin'. Just arguing over the score. As usual."

"But that one guy just punched the other guy."

"Yeah, but if they ain't fightin' yet, they ain't gonna."

"Do they ever get into fights here?"

"Some cats more than others 'cause they used to it. Like Caesar right there, dude that just threw one? I be seeing him uptown all the time—Rucker, Dyckman, Goat Park, and in some of them parks, it ain't no thing to swing. But here, in the Cage, it ain't all about that rah-rah."

"What-what?"

"Rah-rah. Noise. Drama. You ain't from here, huh?"

"My brother and I are here from Herzegovina."

"Hurtsa-go-where? It don't matter, 'cause that's what I'm talking about. Ballers here know that folks come from all over the world to check out the Cage. Everybody wanna see the show."

THE SHOOT

Robert Lipsyte

Looked like a raid. A cop car, flashing lights, no siren, tore down 6th Avenue leading three unmarked white vans. They pulled up along the curb in front of the Cage. Doors banged open; guys piled out. They marched right onto the court. ESPN started screaming at them until the big sergeant waved his arms and yelled, "OK, fellas, that's it. We got next."

Caesar stuck his big face in. "You got . . ." He said the dirty words in Spanish.

A bearded guy with a camera said, "Let's move it, chop-chop, it's magic time."

'Nique said, "Magic time?"

ESPN said, "Must be shootin' a movie. Magic time is about the light." He straightened his shirt and stripped off his goggles.

"It's a PSA," said the cop. "Let's go."

"You can't do this," said 'Nique.

"Just did," said the cop. "Off the court."

"You got a permit?" I said.

Everybody looked at me, hanging on the outside of the fence. I felt hot all over. Nobody ever looked at me down at the Cage, and I didn't know where the words came from.

"Don't need a permit," said the bearded guy. "This is a PSA for the city. You know what PSA stands for?"

"Doesn't matter if it's public service or not," I said. "You can't shoot on city property without the paperwork."

"You some kind of lawyer?" said the cop.

"My dad's a lawyer," I lied. "Everybody knows you need a permit."

I went from hot to cold. Not only was everybody looking at me for the first time, actually listening to me, but it was like I had the ball and they were waiting for me to run the play. I pushed down on my cane to make me taller.

"So let's see the permit," said 'Nique. She turned and winked at me. I went back to hot. That is a girl and a half. I can't even have fantasies about her.

I looked around. Besides the ten ballers on the court, there were about twenty guys from the vans. The ones who weren't carrying equipment were dressed for hoops, but maybe not in the same century. There were old guys with bulging blue veins in their legs and teenagers and superfit guys who looked like they played in those killer lawyer leagues, like Dad did. They were wearing tie-dyes and old-school tight little satins and long NBA unis. I looked at their faces. They all had good haircuts and very white teeth, even the geezers. They were actors.

The bearded guy was tapping his foot and wagging a finger at the cop. "Get it on the road, Kevin. I'm losing the light."

The cop was sweating. "You know," he shouted, "I could run you all for administrative obstruction."

"Then you be back in the Bronx, Kevin," said 'Nique. She looked at me. "What you think, Cane?"

I liked that. I had a name. From her. "I think we need to see the permit."

The cop pulled out a piece of paper and waved it. "Satisfied?"

"No," said 'Nique. She snatched it and pushed it through the fence to me. "This legal?"

My hands were trembling. It was a legal permit all right, but it was for the Happy Warrior Park uptown, the one we called Goat Park. It was where Dad played pick-up and where he started teaching me. I figured something must have happened up there, the drug dealers ran the PSAs off and they came down to the Village to bull their way into the Cage.

"We have a situation," I said.

"You got a solution?" said the bearded guy.

"You talking to that kid?" said the cop.

"Beats talking to you," said the bearded guy. He beckoned to me. "Get in here, Cane."

People got out of my way as I limped along the fence to the opening. It seemed to take a long time, but nobody said anything. People are usually trying to hurry me along or get me out of their way, saying "Excuse me" so nasty it sounds like something Caesar would say to Anglos in Spanish.

It was the first time I'd ever been inside the Cage when there were lots of other people inside. Winter before last, after Dad and I went to a movie across the street, we walked around the empty court and I pretended I was in a game. Dad was pretty weak by then and he had to sag against the fence, but he didn't rush me, he was enjoying watching me. Nobody around but handball players and the *thwack* of three little blue balls against the wall. The tall pale guy called Waco showed up with a basketball, and when it rolled to me, I picked it up at midcourt and drained it. He bounced it back to me and asked me to do that again, and I did. He rebounded and kept feeding me. Six in a row. Dad was nodding and grinning, but he was also sliding down the fence, so I finally tossed the ball back and went to help him. We shuffled out and then down the subway steps outside the Cage. Lots of "Excuse me"s behind us.

The bearded guy came over and shook my hand. "I'm Waldo Monji, the director of this—"

"You directed *Themes*," I said. "Most underrated indie of the year."

His eyes bugged. "I thought no one saw it. What's your name?"

"You can call me Cane." I felt good. *Themes* was underrated because there were only one or two worse films that year. Dad said it gave the word *pretentious* added meaning. We were seeing a lot of movies that last year, about all he could do, and we picked them apart for plot and character. It was quicker than reading novels. Dad was trying to pass along everything he knew while there was time.

"How old are you, Cane?"

If I told him I was sixteen, I'd lose credibility, so I just shook my head as if age was unimportant. I'm not small, and somehow the limp and the cane make me seem older. For sure, makes me feel older.

"So," I said, trying to sound important, "we need to resolve this situation by . . ."

Kevin the Cop and ESPN began growling at the same time. Caesar said, "We ain't moving, so let's play, we —"

"We're not moving, either," said Monji.

"We'll move you," said Caesar. A couple of his cousins came in, as tall as him and wider. The guys from the van pushed closer, and then a couple of hard hats shouldered their way through to back up Caesar's crew. They looked like Indians, American

Indians, the kind who climb high steel. One of them was coughing, that 9/11 hack.

Kevin the Cop unhooked the radio from his belt and lifted it up to his face.

"Hold on," snapped Waco. "We need to resolve this situation right now." The ghost talks! I never heard him say anything much beyond a few words on a break. "Cane, you got a plan?"

I looked around slowly, as if I had a plan. How did I get into this? All the time coming down to the Cage with Dad, then without him, I'd been invisible. We'd work our way to the fence, then hang on it, lost in a live hoops movie. Then go eat somewhere in the Village, maybe see a real movie. After he was gone, I'd come alone but it wasn't the same. Coming to the Cage was about being together, not so much about hoops.

This was going to be my last visit, kind of my private memorial service. I'd been there most of the day, back and forth for food a couple of times, sometimes resting in the jungly park on the uptown side of the court when my leg started throbbing. Interesting day. Some Vietnamese guys I never saw before ran the Cage, and Caesar came close to clocking ESPN for calling him Mira Mira, which is a good nickname for a guy who wants you to look at him, and some chick-o-lattes (as Dad called them) vogued the fence line and this film-school dork made a big deal, like he was Spike instead of Thumbtack, until

'Nique dusted him off. I should have tried to talk to him, offered to gofer. Dad always said writers need to make connections. I could write a movie, excuse me, *film,* for the dork.

"Earth to Cane," said Monji. People laughed. I hadn't heard that line in years.

"OK," I said. "Can't waste magic time. Here's the deal. A compromise. We'll allow Mr. Monji to shoot his PSA." I expected the shouts from the players, so I lifted my cane for quiet. "But one of the teams has to be picked from players on the court. Our players."

Caesar said, "Who elected the handicapped?"

"OK, this is enough," said Kevin the Cop. He started to push people. They pushed back. His hat came off. He raised his radio.

Monji and Waco lifted their arms at the same time. When they spotted each other, they nodded, and I could tell they were going to make my plan happen.

"It's fair," said Waco.

"It's better than fair," said Monji. "It'll look authentic."

"You're gonna need me," said ESPN. He flexed his arms and tightened his jawline. "It wouldn't be . . . authentic . . . without the franchise player."

"He's right," said 'Nique. "More important to look like you got game than to have game."

"No matter what you do, 'Nique," said ESPN, "you not gonna wake up tomorrow with male equipment."

Even the actors started hooting.

I started edging back toward the opening. Get a good spot on the fence to watch this. Took out my cell. I hadn't shot anything since Dad's little speech to me, from his bed, three days before he died. Watched it almost every day for weeks on the bus to school. Dad was looking right down the barrel, saying, "You're smart, you're strong, you can do anything you want, Davey. No limp in your brain. I'm going to be with you all the way. Be kind to Mom and keep taking your best shot."

"Where you going, Cane?" said Waco. "You're our captain. Pick the team."

"Me?"

"Who else?" said 'Nique. She cocked an eyebrow at ESPN, then at Caesar. "Poof Daddy? The Hulk?"

"We're looking for diversity, Cane," said Monji. "Watch me. Actors!"

The hoopsters from the vans lined up. There were about a dozen of them. Monji marched up and down twice. He tapped five of them on the shoulder. A white geezer with a pot belly, an Asian kid my age, a Hispanic guy who looked like a model, a gangsta rapper, and a white woman who looked like one of those skinny tough assistant district attorneys on crime shows.

"Get the idea, Cane?" said Monji. "New York as a

mix of types that can win as a team. The 1970 Knicks, only real people of today's Big Apple."

The ballers crowded around me. 'Nique got really close. I lost a breath until I noticed her skin wasn't so clear. Never been that near to her before. Somehow that made me feel better. She wasn't perfect either.

I stepped back, looked them over. I knew every one of them, their moves, what they could and couldn't do on the court. Knew things about them they didn't even know, since Dad and I talked about them, made up stories for them on the subway home. I loved that part of the trip most of all, Dad coming up with a detail, then throwing it to me.

Why you think 'Nique always keeps space around her, elbows and knees out? Nobody gets close even though she's fast enough to fake. She's afraid of contact, I said. *Maybe she's been beat up. I like that,* said Dad. *If you're going to be a writer, you have to be thinking like that all the time.*

ESPN, he would say, why does he need attention so much? I'd say, Lack of self-esteem? OK, Dad would say, but why? What's going on in his life? I'd say, He lives in a rathole, he's not smart, basketball's his only ticket out, and he's not so sure his ticket is gonna get punched. Dad would laugh and say, Not as dumb as you look.

Dad and I got tight around basketball. Those last two years were the best. Mom says it's sad he had to be dying to become intimate with his own son, but she's still bitter about him. When we all lived together on the West Side, he was never around, teaching at the college or writing in his office. In good weather he'd be in Goat Park around the corner on Amsterdam or uptown at Rucker or the Kingdome. In the winter he'd be in a gym somewhere banging away, usually in those tough lawyer leagues where he was good enough to be a ringer. Dad started in high school and came off the bench in college, and he had hopes for me until the accident. Mom said he felt guilty about that; he was supposed to be watching me instead of playing when I wandered out in front of a couple of kids racing bikes. I was eight. I heard I was lucky to keep the leg.

"Let's go," said ESPN. "This ain't the NBA draft."

"The light, Cane, the light," said Monji.

It wasn't hard. Maybe not exactly the team Dad would have picked—we talked about that, too—but a good team, with diversity. ESPN, 'Nique, Caesar, and Waco. Black, woman, Hispanic, and very white. The fifth was the hard choice. I was trying to decide between Boo and Red. Their games were about the same. Then I spotted the Indian guy, his hard hat under his arm.

"What's your name?" I said.

He glanced at Waco and gave me a funny grin. "Cochise."

"You're on," I said.

He shook his head a little apologetically and thumped his chest. "Don't have a full game in me."

"Not a full game," said Waco. "Need an outside shooter."

"You guys ready?" said Monji.

"We want Equity rates," said ESPN. "Same as your guys getting."

"It's a PSA," said Monji. "We're all waiving our fees."

"Be your audition, E," said 'Nique. "For *Zombie Hoops.*"

"I like that. You be the monster."

The guys with cameras and sound booms, some of them girls, took positions around the court and the makeup and hair ladies started powdering and combing. Monji said something about Waco being too pale, but before anyone could slap powder on his face, Waco walked away. ESPN wanted his eyebrows darkened, and 'Nique got in a big discussion about her hair. The actors were mostly made up already, just needed touch-ups.

A girl came around with a clipboard and asked my team to sign papers.

"What's this?" said Caesar.

"Release forms," she said.

"For permission to use your image," I said. "You don't have to use your real name."

The girl shot me a nasty look, but then Monji started yelling and she shrugged.

Monji rushed them through warm-ups, then stepped off the court. "Play ball."

I got behind the backboard on the uptown side so I could lean against the fence there if I had to.

The assistant-DA type said, "Three-pointers?"

"No," said Monji. "Too hard to edit."

"Yes," said Waco. "You want authentic?"

"You guys always play treys?" said Monji.

"Yes," I lied so Waco wouldn't have to. He looked at me with those dark dead eyes. I could only imagine he was grateful. But imagine is what I do, bro.

Monji glanced up at the sky, sighed, shrugged, nodded.

They won the toss; the Geezer took it out.

Monji's guys could play, but they couldn't really play together. They tried stuff that would look good if it worked, alley-oop passes for on-your-head dunks, but you can't do that if you haven't practiced it. They had enough trouble with picks. They wanted to look good. Those PSAs are short; getting a couple seconds of screen time is a big deal. It could lead to a commercial, a role in a lousy Monji film. The Hispanic model could slash to the hoop, but only if no one was in his path, and 'Nique always got at least one butt cheek in front of him. The rapper was their big man, fearless, but he was slow and he couldn't go all the way up with Waco. Cochise did a good job boxing him out until he started coughing, and then he just waited for an outside shot. By the time the actors pulled ahead, 6–4, ESPN was playing a half-court game because he was a dog, and Cochise was always a step behind, breathing through his mouth.

'Nique, Waco, and Caesar kept us in the game. I started feeling something like love for them, without even liking them very much. 'Nique was a warrior, no one was going to get over her, and Caesar had a mean streak, he just wanted to chop you down, and Waco's steady game never wavered, never quit. He passed a lot. He ran without the ball.

Dad always said, You've got to have a mystery character in your story, one that's going to surprise the reader. Who would it be? He was trying to finish a book before he died, but he didn't make it. It was a basketball thriller — he wrote mostly literary detective novels that didn't make much money — and he said he would turn it over to me if he got too sick. He did, but I haven't been able to open it yet.

I could hear Dad saying, So who is the mystery character here?

Has to be Waco, with his ghostly look, his dead calm, and his weird tats.

Too obvious, said Dad. That boy's been in Iraq or Afghanistan or both, killed people, seen buddies die, maybe got hurt himself. He plays ball to keep the demons out of his head, to forget the Haj. He's no mystery except to himself.

So who's the mystery man?

It's always the writer, said Dad. The one with the power to thrill, to teach, to surprise. Writer always gets the last shot.

Cochise went down. He was on his hands and knees, coughing and retching, until two hard hats came on the court and lifted him up. As they led him off, Cochise looked around and said, "Sorry."

"Sub him," yelled Monji.

Waco pointed at me. "Cane."

I jerked off the back fence into a gray-taped backboard pole. "Me?"

"Be four against five," said ESPN.

"Like life," said 'Nique.

"We want to win," said Caesar.

"Not about winning or losing," said Monji. "It's about making a movie. I like this. A gutsy crippled guy."

"We need an outside shooter," said Waco. "I've seen his game."

"Where?" I started to remember.

"Here. You were with an old dude. Your grandfather?"

"Dad," I said. "He was real sick." I felt I needed to explain.

"He was proud of you," said Waco.

"How'd you know that?" I wanted to hear more.

"Later." Waco waved me on-court. "Stay in the game. Be ready."

"For what?"

The game went on around me, without me. I was an invisible spectator again, only this time I was inside the fence, on the court. It looked like four against five, but the model and the Geezer and the rapper were sucking air while Waco and 'Nique and Caesar were just getting stronger, tougher. They wanted to win; this was their court; they were going to beat back the invaders, reclaim their land. I wanted to share this with Dad; it was the key to our story. Hoops was their life; it was all they had right now, maybe would ever have unless the game gave them confidence for something else. Tonight I am going to open Dad's manuscript, finish his book for him.

"Stay in the game, Cane," yelled Waco.

The actors were leading, 10–9, and 'Nique was shouting, "Got to win by two," when the assistant DA slapped the ball out of ESPN's hand and bounced it through Caesar's legs to the Asian kid, who fired it to the rapper, who shouldered to the basket, traveling all the way. He went straight up. Waco went up with him. Black and white arms rising to the hoop.

Waco punched the ball out of the rapper's hand, right to me at half court.

I am all alone because I am invisible, the writer,

the mystery character. As Dad taught me, I soften my hands for the impact of the ball, take it in, grind the grit into my fingers, then lighten the touch until only my fingertips control the ball. I flex the good leg, relax the bad leg, lift my arms, and let the ball go. I follow the thought straight to the end of the story.

AFTERWORD

Marc Aronson

Readers, I had more time to write this little piece than I expected. Last Friday I went to the gym to play some ball. I found three guys, and we started a good game of two-on-two—I made a couple of nice drives and we'd just come back from being down 7–3 to tying the score when I felt like someone threw a hardball and bashed me in the leg. I had been bad—hadn't stretched, wasn't in shape, and tore my Achilles tendon. I should have known better: the combined ages of the other three people on the court was less than mine. I am seriously old. But if you love the game, you just love the game. It is in your blood. For now, I can't play—all I can do is read, and write, basketball stories.

When you walk out on a basketball court, you walk into a story: I win; you lose. But that's only the big picture: every move you see has a story behind it. No, many stories. When you shoot a jump shot just right, you don't have to look; you *know* it's good—and that's because of the hundred, no, thousand, times you've shot it, and when it feels that golden, that pure, it always goes through—nothing but net. Sometimes you pattern yourself on a star you see on TV—so you are literally reenacting history, trying to be what you saw. But then some of those practices were with coaches—in school, or on a team. That coach taught you how to slide your feet on D, how to box out, how to follow through—leaving that gooseneck arch of fingers hanging in the air. Your coach was passing on a layer of history—lessons from an earlier generation. Maybe there is even a trace of old James Naismith in some of those drills—the guy who invented basketball in December of 1891. But when you come to play pick-up, street ball, especially in a big city, there is yet another mist of history around you: the stories of the legends, the men who walked on air.

In Willie's and Bob Burleigh's and Joe's stories, they mention some legends of the game: Joe "the Destroyer" Hammond, Earl "the Goat" Manigault, Spanish Doc, Corky, Helicopter, Pee Wee Kirkland, Smush Parker, and former Knick Anthony Mason. Those are (or were) real people, who really did amazing things. There have been black players on college teams forever—though for a long time that was mainly in historically black colleges and a few northern schools. Major college basketball began to be integrated only in 1947, and the NBA followed three years later. But there was a long period, from the 1950s clear up to the '70s, when some colleges resisted having black students and even integrated college and pro teams made sure to remain predominantly white. These racist policies left a great many terrific players behind to play street ball. And that was not so bad. The street heroes had enthusiastic fans, they could wow the crowds, and they could even pick up a lot of money — legally or illegally. The college and pro recruiters were nervous about the players — and the players were not so eager to give up the streets. So the official college and pro stats are only part of the history of the game. The other part is the legends.

The most famous street-ball tournament was organized by Holcombe Rucker, a New York City playground director. The Rucker contests of the '60s are so famous, people still talk about them. You can see (or play in) Rucker, Gaucho, and Riverside tournaments today, though Rucker is not on the original playground. The good news is that these great players have been described in some terrific books. That is yet another way that walking out on a court is walking into a story — if you love playing, there is so much worth reading. The classics are Pete Axthelm's *The City Game,* Rick Telander's *Heaven Is a Playground,* and Darcy Frey's *The Last Shot.* But I've also seen some newer books and even videos on the Rucker, or the Goat, or the mingled history of civil rights and basketball. And to be personal, the first piece I ever published was an op-ed in the *New York Times* — about the sad day when the two courts where I used to play pick-up ball were closed and I realized how much those games meant to me ("Melting Court, Melting Pavement," July 4, 1987).

Charles and I created this book as a way to get some of the feeling of pick-up on the page. So we made the book itself a kind of game. We chose the setting and the date and gave each author a time slot. Each author knew who was on the court because we didn't let an author write a new story until the previous one was done. Each writer came on the court knowing who was playing, who had won, but ready to tell his or her own story. And that is just what it is in pick-up — there is the constant of the game and the court, but the ever changing challenge of the mix of players and skills that you find when it is your next. Nothing could be more fun. One day I was standing with my older son at a court in Venice Beach, California — body builders and strange creatures on roller skates all around us. We found a game, just as we usually do at our local Jewish center in suburban New Jersey. The two games could not have been more different, or more similar. And in a way, that's what the stories in this book are — similar and totally different. I hope some of you try your own pick-up games — choose a place, a time, set the rules of the game, and start to tell stories — just the way you do on the court.

Marc Aronson is an editor and author of many award-winning books for young people, including *Master of Deceit: J. Edgar Hoover and America in the Age of Lies; War Is . . . : Soldiers, Survivors, and Storytellers Talk About War,* which he coedited with Patty Campbell; and *Sugar Changed the World: A Story of Magic, Spice, Slavery, Freedom, and Science,* which he cowrote with Marina Budhos. His book *Sir Walter Ralegh and the Quest for El Dorado* won the Robert F. Sibert Medal and a *Boston Globe–Horn Book* Award. Marc Aronson lives in New Jersey.

Bruce Brooks is the author of two hoops books: *The Moves Make the Man,* a novel, and *Those Who Love the Game,* the true story of Celtics coach Doc Rivers's life in the NBA and elsewhere. Bruce has written other books too, many of them about sports. He has three sons and lives in Brooklyn.

Joseph Bruchac has had a lifelong love of basketball, even though he was too short to make the team his first three years in high school. (He explores that time in another of his stories, "Swish," which was anthologized in *Lay-Ups and Long Shots.*) He also feels a special connection to the game because of his American Indian ancestry. Ball games of all kinds were played by many Native American nations before the coming of Europeans, and the rubber ball was an invention of the peoples of Central America.

Robert Burleigh says, "There have been countless alleys, garage driveways, playgrounds, YMCAs, sports clubs, school gyms. I wish I could remember all the names and cool (and not so cool) nicknames I've carried in my head. It would be nice to have a few videos, too, because some people I played with had real game. What remains most for me, though, is the feeling of moving on the fly (3 on 2, 2 on 1, whatever) when the flow — no matter what part of it you are — is pure magic. That, along with the rough of the ball in your hands, won't soon go. My one attempt to catch the game in words is a picture book called *Hoops*, published in the late '90s by Harcourt, and illustrated by Steven Johnson."

Sharon G. Flake has one of the most authentic voices in young adult literature today. From elementary school through college, young people, educators, and school districts across the nation clamor for her work. She is a multiple Coretta Scott King Award winner whose novel *The Skin I'm In* made her a household name. Her collection *You Don't Even Know Me: Short Stories and Poems About Boys* demonstrates her ability to captivate male readers and speak to their hopes and concerns. Sharon G. Flake's claim to basketball is the hoop attached to her house. It was there when she purchased the home eleven years ago and has been used sparingly. "Since I never did use that hoop or follow basketball, I had to put my own spin on the basketball story I wrote for this collection, proving that at a game, all the action doesn't take place on the court."

Robert Lipsyte is a longtime sports and city columnist for the *New York Times*. He is also the author of the young adult novels *The Contender, One Fat Summer,* and *Center Field.* In 2001, he won the Margaret A. Edwards Award from the American Library Association for lifetime contribution to young adult literature. While he grew up in New York believing that one-wall handball was the true city game, he never lost his deadly underhand free throw. Because of his enormous respect, he will never dunk on Walter Dean Myers.

Walter Dean Myers says, "My best basketball experience: getting into a game with Wilt Chamberlain, who had brought a crew up from Philly to play at (I believe) City College. I was a 160-pound guard, and Wilt was Wilt. I got caught in a switch and found myself behind him in the lane. He backed in—his butt in my chest—and called for the ball. I decided to make a joke of it and grabbed his arm. Wilt got the ball and went up, lifting me off the ground. A lesson in understanding levels of basketball. I also traveled to Prague to watch basketball there and used the city as the origin of one player in my book *Game.* Seymour Simon's late wife (a fanatical Knicks fan) set me up to meet local Czechs." Walter Dean Myers is one of the most important writers for children today. His books include the much-lauded *Monster, Fallen Angels, Sunrise over Fallujah,* and, most recently, *Riot.*

Willie Perdomo is the author of *Where a Nickel Costs a Dime* and *Smoking Lovely,* which received a PEN America Beyond Margins Award. He has also been published in the *New York Times Magazine, Bomb, African Voices,* and *CENTRO journal.* His children's book *Visiting Langston* received a Coretta Scott King Honor, and his most recent picture book is called *Clemente!* He has been a Pushcart Prize nominee and a Woolrich Fellow in Creative Writing at Columbia University and a New York Foundation for the Arts Poetry Fellow. He is cofounder and publisher of Cypher Books.

Adam Rapp has been a full-fledged basketball junkie since the age of nine. In addition to playing high-school, college, semipro, and pro ball, he has played in all the major unlimited and pro-am tournaments in New York City, including the West

4th Summer Classic, where he was twice selected to the all-star team. He currently plays five times a week and can still go by guys half his age. He is the author of several YA novels, including the Michael L. Printz Honor winner *Punkzilla*.

Charles R. Smith Jr. says, "Basketball has been good to me. I've loved the game for as long as I can remember, and it has provided me with endless stories, poetry, and photographs that have filled many of my books, including this one. When I moved to NYC from my native California, the street game caught my eye. I carried my ball and camera with me everywhere, from Soul in the Hole in Brooklyn, to Rucker in Harlem, to West 4th Street in Manhattan. I took pictures of modern playground legends like Main Event, Booger, Future, Alimoe the Black Widow, and future NBA players like Smush Parker and Ron Artest, just to name a few. I photographed all of them plying their trade and scribbled notes when a particularly interesting nickname or piece of dialogue was exchanged and saved it for later. Well, now is later and all that time spent on my feet has provided me with a career in books. I have plenty of books on other topics, but when it comes to ball, that's a well that never runs dry."

Charles R. Smith Jr. is the author of several books for children, including the Coretta Scott King Honor winner *Twelve Rounds to Glory: The Story of Muhammad Ali* and the Coretta Scott King Award winner *My People*, along with plenty of books on basketball, including *Rimshots, Short Takes, Hoop Queens, Hoop Kings,* and, for the youngest of readers, *Let's Play Basketball!*

Rita Williams-Garcia says, "When I was taking dance classes in the West Village, I'd pass crowds hanging on to the chain-link fence watching the action inside the Cage. Sometimes I'd watch the run. Mostly I'd scan the onlookers who couldn't pull away from the spectacular plays and the on-court brutality. When I was writing my novel *Jumped*, I wanted Dominique to be a point guard and to know something about that kind of brutality. In one chapter she mentions playing ball on 4th Street. It was a no-brainer to suit Dominique up when I was invited to contribute a story to *Pick-Up Game*. Not only did I want to get a girl inside the Cage; I also wanted to get that collision of West Village art and the physical contest inside the Cage. With the IFC Center directly opposing the Cage on 6th Avenue, I had to go for it. As a girl playing ball in my neighborhood, my shooting wasn't great, but I could dribble, pass, and guard. Even today while bouncing from game to game on cable, I stay glued to whoever's playing guard. My all-time favorite guard in the WNBA is the late Kim Perrot of the Houston Comets."